CATURDAY KNIFE SPECIAL

CADDY CAT CAFE' MYSTERIES

CJ REYNOLDS

LAUREL LANE PRESS

CJReynoldsAuthor.com

Sign up for Newsletter

https://cjreynoldsauthor.com/newsletter/

Grab a large copy of these plans in the back of the book.

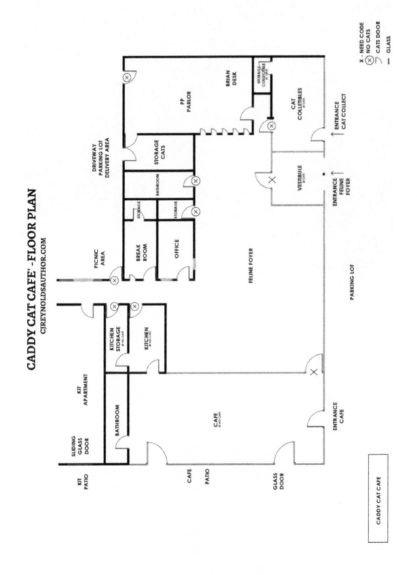

Dad & Gram, this is for you.

CHAPTER I

She drove into the Caddy Cat Café's parking lot but immediately slammed on the brakes. She turned off the engine and stepped outside the car. The drive from San Francisco to here sucked. Weeks of crappy takeout food, sleepless nights, and miles of long, boring roads with nothing to do but spin the hell of this past year's mistakes in her head.

Exhausted, but she made it, finally. Misty Bottom Cove, Massachusetts, the home of Caddy Cat Café and now the continuation of her living hell.

The last hour's drive was tough. She had wanted the journey from San Francisco to here to be over and thought what she would do when she got here. She planned it all. A quick hello to the staff, especially Sarah at the café, get the keys, and head to the apartment. She'd then call Tess, her best friend who she hadn't seen in years, and chill for the evening.

But this was not expected.

"You have got to be kidding me!"

Staring at the building, her mouth open, her focus narrowed as she ran her hands over her head, and her ponytail loosened as her red hair fell loosely over her shoulders.

"This place is massive! Holy shit!"

Seven years ago, it was a tiny café with no cats. *What have I got myself into?* she thought, as she looked at all the cars in the parking lot, the people walking in and out. Her mind raced.

But it was beautiful. Dark yellow stucco with dark brown trim. The place was full of windows. The sign was a silhouette of a cat licking its paw above the name Caddy Cat Café in fancy script.

The café was on the end of a long strip and took up most of the building, except for a small real estate office on the other end. The café wrapped around the left side, where a patio, wood beams, and a trellis faced the ocean.

"This place is not *quaint.*"

The outside tables were full of customers, some pounding at their keyboards, others talking and laughing. A few people were ready to run down the ocean path parallel to the building.

In the windows, she could see an orange cat walking across the windowsill, its collar glistening from the sun. A gray cat snoozed on a hammock.

Kit's mouth was still gaping. Her palms were sweaty, her legs wobbly. Her mind was still racing.

"It's too big. It's too much. What if I can't...? Damn it, Nan!"

She jumped up and down, yelling into her palms before she crunched them into fists. She kicked a few pebbles that went flying around the parking lot.

Finally, Kit turned around and faced the street to catch her breath. With her eyes closed, she breathed, then unclenched her fists, adjusted her sweater, and squared her shoulders.

"Crap," she said, turning back around to face a huge building full of people looking at her. They quickly scurried away from the window. Her little hissy fit had been in full view.

"Seriously, Kit, this place is all windows," she said to herself. "Pull it together."

She went to the building's main entrance. To the right, with a separate door, was a shop with a big yellow sign: Kitty Cat Collectibles. A smaller sign read, "Unique collectibles made by local artists for your furry friends."

She walked into the building but found herself in a small windowed lobby facing a second door that was locked. A woman from Kitty Cat Collectibles walked around and opened it.

"Kit, your grandmother told me you were coming. Welcome." She winked and went back to a customer in the shop.

There were cats everywhere. A wide open room to her left was filled with cat boxes, cat trees, elevated catwalks, and cubbies. For humans, there were tall tables, high-back chairs, and a couple of small couches. The entire left wall was a gigantic window separating the cats from the café.

An upholstered bench and more cat perches were against the window.

At the back of the room, on the left side of the hallway, there was a door to a kitchen with plexiglass at the bottom so no one would hit the cats going in and out.

"Plexiglass? Hmmm. Nan thought of everything."

A few baristas in green aprons were in the cats' area, which, according to a sign, was the Feline Foyer, but most were in the café serving food and coffee. Cat handlers wore shirts with the Caddy Cat Café insignia in the corner.

There was an office across from the kitchen with a window facing forward and left into the Feline Foyer. To the right, there were rows of small cat doors that allowed the cats to enter the PP Parlor.

Good place to go to get away from touchy-feely humans.

A few customers mingled with the cats. One woman was chased as she dragged a feather on a stick around the table. Her kids laughed at the jumping cat.

So many cats—too many to count. But then again, it had been years since she had been around so many.

"Kit, I'm so glad you're here!" A short blonde girl bounced over to her, coming in for a hug.

"Sarah? You look so much older," she said.

They walked over to a small counter at the back of the Feline Foyer near the kitchen. She could hear pans clanking.

"Well, yeah, we met when I started here. I was still in high school. Seven years later, I'm still here," Sarah said, looking around, smiling. "We have so much to talk about." Her voice was bubbly, her blue eyes sparkling.

"Yes, we do." Kit leaned her arm over the counter.

Sarah squinted at Kit. "You must be exhausted."

Kit smiled and closed one eye. "How could you tell?"

"Would you like a cup of my special coffee?"

Kit blew out a breath. "Yes, that would be lovely."

Sarah nodded, and Kit followed her. They entered the door with the plexiglass bottom, and Kit noticed a young brown-haired woman putting pastries in the oven and a thin guy, who seemed to be rambling on about a football game, washing dishes. Both paused for a moment in silence as they followed Kit with their eyes.

Sarah and Kit went through another set of doors on the other side to enter the café area. Like a long galley, it spread from where they stood to the front of the building. It was basically an oversized fish aquarium. All windows. You could choose to look out toward the patio and the ocean or turn one-eighty for cat entertainment. Win-win.

High counters facing the ocean extended the entire length of the café. The chairs were dark brown with a cat emblem on the back, and the tables were round in a lighter color. The chatter was low as most seemed to be working on their computers or on their phones.

Turning back to the coffee bar, which butted up against the windows of the Feline Foyer, Sarah walked behind the counter and started making magic. She moved like a dancer around another barista who was pulling something delicious from a microwave.

Glancing up, Kit noticed a white cat peeking out of a box mounted to the foyer side of the window.

Kit slid into a comfortable high-back chair at the counter.

"Who is that cutie up there?" She nodded her head toward the cat.

Sarah peeked her head around the coffee machine.

"Daisy," Sarah yelled over the loud coffee maker. "Daisy is our spoiled girl. She's not too bright, but she's adorable." Pointing to her head, "See the mark on her forehead? It looks like a daisy. Watch out for her. She likes to get under your feet."

Sarah poured the coffee into a cup and placed it in front of Kit.

"She's sweet, but she thinks she's a princess."

She handed Kit a lid for the cup. "Here, put this on your coffee, so we can go back to see the cats."

Kit and Sarah walked to a glass door at the left end of the café. Sarah pressed in a code and looked at Kit. "Most of our doors have codes. No one can come in here without paying. I'll get you your code and keys later."

As they walked into the Feline Foyer, Daisy made a soft cooing noise as she jumped ten feet to the bench below.

Sarah stopped. "And...Daisy can jump."

Kit leaned back. "I guess so."

They both sat on the bench as Kit pet the cat.

"People can bring their coffee in here, but they must cover it with a lid," Sarah said as she leaned over to rub Daisy's head too.

"I'll get you a book about the cat rules. The biggest one is that patrons aren't supposed to pick up the cats. We can. One of the perks of working here."

Kit took a slow sip of her coffee. "Ah, this is good, Sarah. Where did you get your skills?"

Sarah gave a big smile. "My secret. What I want to know is what happened in the parking lot? You looked like you were freaking out."

Kit looked down at Daisy. She rubbed the cat's chin, focusing on the purring for a moment.

"It's something I must work on. Which I am." She smiled.

"That's good. I'll do what I can to help, but I see this is something you'll have to figure out on your own."

Kit smiled. "This coffee is amazing. Come on, what is this secret?" Kit said, looking back up smiling.

Sarah smiled too.

CHAPTER 2

K it enjoyed sitting and watching the cats after Sarah went back to work. It amazed her how different Sarah was. Now she was a confident girl who loved what she did. A wave of jealousy hit Kit in the gut as she realized how nice it would be to have her shit together.

A loud voice boomed at the end of the bench. "What the...?"

Kit turned around and noticed a girl plastered against a seat. A woman close to her pointed her finger, yelling. The girl's wide eyes darted around; her blue hair stuck to the glass wall.

The gray-haired woman wagged her stubby arms and fat fingers closer and closer to the girl's face.

Even more disturbing was the small orange cat the girl held on to. The cat's eyes squinted, ears pulled back, as it attempted to bury itself in the girl's arms.

"Oh no, you don't," Kit said under her breath. She dropped her bag on the floor and beelined it toward the woman.

The cat was terrified and the girl, well, she looked ready to cry. As Kit got closer, she could hear the woman shout.

"I will toss you out! You will never see Peanut Butter again. Do you hear me?"

Tears welled up in the girl's eyes as she gripped the cat closer. Unable to hold it back, she sobbed.

"You're scaring Peannnut Butttter. You are sooo mean," she whimpered between gasps.

"This is the last warning. Next time, you will be gone," the woman said, an air of delight in her voice.

The woman turned to walk away with a smirk on her face, but Kit stood right there.

She looked Kit up and down.

"Excuse me," she snapped as she moved to the right.

Kit moved to block her. This woman was shorter than Kit, and her expression was full of hurt or hate. Maybe both. Her jawline was thick, and the muscles protruded when she spoke. Plus, she had short arms and a round body. She looked like a T-rex.

Before the other woman could speak again, Kit raised her voice. "Yes, I am definitely in your way. Who the hell do you think you are, yelling at her like that?"

"Excuse me?"

"You heard me, and I asked you a question."

The T-rex lowered her voice to a growl. "You need to get out of my way before I remove you from this building."

"Ha! I'd like to see you try."

"I am the manager and—"

"Not for long," Kit said and crossed her arms.

"I'm calling the police to have you removed." The woman pulled her phone out.

Kit laughed and moved closer to look at her name badge. "It will be your last phone call, Ms. . . .Ms. Marjorie Pigeon. The manager. Interesting." Kit clucked her tongue.

Marjorie puffed her chest, standing firm.

"Kit! Kit!" Sarah yelled from across the room as she sprinted over.

Marjorie straightened and her face lost color fast. Kit thought, *So this is what a pale dinosaur would look like. Hmmm.*

"You're Nan's granddaughter?" Marjorie asked, her voice catching.

Kit leaned forward, glaring at Marjorie, almost with a sense of delight. "Yes," she said. "We are going to talk in the office. Right. Now."

Marjorie's eyes widened, but she pushed her gray hair back and stood still.

Leaning closer to Kit, she said, "Well, you could have told me who you are. You didn't have to play games."

Kit looked up at the ceiling, held her breath, and gritted her teeth. "You will be out of a job in about twenty minutes if you don't get into that office right now."

Marjorie twitched slightly, but she squared her shoulders, huffed, and walked to the office.

The girl with the cat grinned and continued to rub Peanut Butter's head.

Kit winked at her and turned to look at Marjorie's back end.

Look at her. She walks as if she owns the place.

If only...*Hey, Marjorie! She turned around. Kit lifted a bat and swung hard. The bat cracked the woman's head upon impact. Blood squirted out of the wound, and a bit of brain matter landed on the floor. The look of horror on Marjorie's face made Kit smile. Kit called the girl with the cat to come over and take a swing.*

"Kit?" Sarah nudged her.

"Oh, sorry. I was thinking about something."

"I don't think I've ever heard anyone talk to her like that. That was awesome," Sarah said with a chuckle. She then looked around. "Tsk-tsk. Kit, you made a scene again."

"She made me angry. She's a bully." Kit shrugged and walked over to the girl, but for a moment, she considered the irony of the situation.

Am I a bully too? Nah, I'm just protecting the innocent.

The girl's fading blue hair was still stuck to her cheek.

"What's your name?"

"Leanne," she whispered.

"She will never talk to you like that again. I promise," Kit said.

Leanne pulled Peanut Butter in close and smiled. A sweet childlike smile. Peanut Butter purred.

Kit walked into the office and realized she couldn't wait to clean it. Boxes in every corner, overstuffed shelves full of paperwork probably from five years ago. Even the couch had stuff piled high with who knows what. There was crap everywhere, including a few empty cups and old food wrappers. It reminded her of college. Trying to refocus, she looked at Marjorie, whose back was to her.

Marjorie turned around. Her beady eyes squinted, which pushed them together. They looked dark, like black buttons—no expression. Add this to her rolling, wrinkled face and jutting-out chin, and she really did look like a T-rex. *Not an expression of concern at all. Just fake, like her personality.*

Marjorie put her hand out. "It's nice to meet you. I'm glad you're here. I didn't mean to sound rude to you, but I needed to take care of that situation." When Kit didn't take her hand, Marjorie turned back around and lowered her voice. "That girl is inappropriate and has been causing some, um, issues."

Kit stood with her arms crossed. "Cut the shit, Marjorie. I'm not playing your game. *You* were inappropriate and caused, um, some issues."

Marjorie pointed out the office window at Leanne. "That girl has been putting the cat in her backpack. She's hoarding it, and that's against our policy. I've been here for years, and your grandmother likes how I run a tight ship. I always follow policy. She appreciates my ability to keep this place running. I ask you, what would happen if everyone put the cats in their backpack? Would they steal them? Would they suffocate? You didn't think of that, did you?" Marjorie asked.

"Are you done with the drama? Where in the policy does it tell you to yell at a girl and make her cry? Please show me that policy." Kit felt her anger rise. *Keep it together,* she kept repeating in her mind.

Marjorie ignored her. "She gets mad when anyone else is around the cat. She's here every day and hasn't been sharing the cat, and she pays nothing. Never has because of some rule that was put in years ago. Plus, you know, she really needs to brush her hair," she said, nodding in Leanne's direction.

"I see," Kit said as she adjusted her shirt and bit her lip. *Keep it together, Kit.*

Again, Marjorie ignored her. "You should trust my judgment. You know, I—"

"Just stop!" Kit barked.

Marjorie's jaw muscle twitched. Kit turned and faced the window, standing next to Marjorie. She looked at the cat and Leanne enjoying their time together. "You had that cat terrified, and that is unacceptable."

Marjorie pushed her chin out further. "She's hoarding the cat. It's our policy to not hoard cats. I had every right."

Kit spoke slowly. "No. You have no right to yell at anyone in public."

"You yelled at me! Ha! Hypocrite much?"

"You're going there? Really?" Kit faced Marjorie's T-rex profile. "You will *not* have a job if this keeps up. Do I make myself clear?"

Marjorie tightened. Her face was now red, and her jaw taut. Kit felt her own pulse bounding in her neck. She didn't move at all.

"This is my office. I have some work to do," Marjorie finally said.

"That's fine. Do your work," Kit said as she turned to the door. "One more thing. Please clean this office. It looks like a college dorm room, and we're gonna share it. I don't want a messy roommate. I'll be moving my stuff in here on Sunday, so you have till Saturday."

Kit closed the door as the venetian blinds snapped down with a bang. Something else fell from the couch onto the floor.

Kit noticed a few staff members scurry around, acting busy. Kit met Sarah, picked up her cold coffee, and tried to ignore her shaky hands. She took a breath and sat down. Out of the corner of her eye she saw a tall lanky, kid knock on Marjorie's office and walk in. "Who is that?" Kit pointed.

"Peter. Marjorie took him under her wing. He's okay, but he can't get out of his own way."

A moment later, Peter walked out, glaring at Kit.

"It seems they share the same dagger stare." Sarah paused, watching Peter almost trip over a cat. "Listen," Sarah said in a whisper. "I know I'm overstepping my boundaries, but be careful with Marjorie. She can be vindictive. You're on her radar now."

"Good times. Have you seen that office?" Kit asked, pretending to shiver as she adjusted herself in the seat. "I have to share an office with her. I'll probably find a mouse in my coffee."

Sarah giggled. "Too many cats here. Never happen."

"Still, I'm afraid of what's in there. Besides Marjorie, of course."

On the other side of the room, she watched a tall man walk out of a door near the Kitty Cat Collectibles carrying a small black and white cat. Her eyes widened. He must've been over six feet five with messy reddish-brown hair and big blue eyes. His beard complimented his smile. He wore a black T-shirt that said "Biker's Best Sidekick" with a picture of a cat wearing a motorcycle helmet. A few of the patrons walked over to him to pet the cat or maybe to inspect the man.

"Sarah, who is that?" Kit asked

"Oh, that's Brian, our head cat handler."

"That's Brian? Nan loves Brian. I heard the cats do too."

"Yeah, he's amazing at what he does. The cats flock to him," she said as she tipped her head down.

"Do I detect someone is smitten?" Kit said, bumping her shoulder into Sarah.

Flushing, she dropped her gaze.

"He's here early every morning and stays late at night. Marjorie hired him because she said he was cute. Her words. He gives her a run for her money, though. He's the one person who is never on her radar. At least not in that way. Years ago, she would order his supplies late, so he had to come in on his days off. He figured out her game and told me that no one messes with his cats."

"I bet he means it too," Kit said.

"Just last week, Brian got into an argument about the ordering being slow again. He kept putting sticky notes on her computer, but she waited until the last minute to get the cat litter ordered. This is the stuff she does. Luckily, Brian had extra hidden stock."

"Sarah, that door Brian came out of. That's where the litter and food is, right?"

"Yes, we call it the PP Parlor. Cat food, litter, and a place for the cats to rest, away from the people. They also get their checkups back there. Brian was a vet tech, so he does most of that. He's thinking of going back to college to be a veterinarian. I hope he does. He's so good with animals."

Kit laughed. "PP Parlor, that's funny. Did Nan come up with that?"

"Of course," Sarah said.

"You still haven't answered my question."

Sarah waved at Brian.

He walked around the room, talking to the patrons. The black and white cat jumped to the floor as kids waited to play with it. He finally arrived in front of Sarah and Kit.

"Hey, you must be Kit. I'm Brian." He extended a hand the size of a baseball glove.

She shook his hand. "Nice to meet you. My grandmother spoke highly of you."

"I love Nan. She's brilliant and a hoot! We always have so much fun working together," he said.

Kit waved her finger. "She is. But she is also sneaky. She didn't mention the size of this building."

"Really? Yeah, it has expanded a lot, especially in the past two years. I'm having a hard time keeping up with the changes."

Kit leaned back to look up at Brain. "I thought you were the cat handler?"

Brain chuckled. "I wear many helmets. Cat handler, builder, coffee maker... well, I'm better at building than making coffee."

Sarah leaned into Kit. "He's right about that."

Brian looked down at Sarah and smiled. Then he leaned in toward Kit. "I heard you met Marjorie."

"Oh, were we that loud?"

He shrugged and made a waffling movement with his hand.

"Um, sorry about that. I need to control my ang... frustration."

"She brings out the best in people. Don't sweat it."

Sarah watched Brian walk away. She smiled, and her cheeks flushed.

"Sarah, do you have my keys from Nan?"

Patting her green smock, she pulled out an envelope and handed it to Kit.

"I'll get you the codes later." Sarah pointed to a hall past the office. "The apartment is down the hall, the door on the left across from the window. Nan was tired of going out and around, so she put in a door back there. We cleared the area out for you."

"Convenient. Nan loves to keep things simple. I'm going to get settled for a while. How late will you be here?"

"I leave at eight. I'll work at the counter until four. My new girl will take over while I help Brian move a few cat boxes. See those landing boxes on the wall? They're too far apart.

The older cats can't jump it, so we're going to add another wave board so they can walk it."

"Okay, sounds good. I've planned a meeting with the staff tomorrow at nine. Can you let everyone know? It's not mandatory. I just want to meet the staff."

"Yup, I will. Kit, it's great to have you here," Sarah said as she half-hugged Kit.

CHAPTER 3

Kit turned around to head to her apartment, but found herself face-to-face with an orange cat inches from her nose. Kit gasped and almost fell backward.

The girl with the blue hair held the orange cat in the air. "P-p-Peanut -B-Butter thanks y-you," she said slowly.

As she lowered the cat, Kit saw her smile. Leanne was shorter than she looked sitting down. Round in her face and belly, her hair was still matted, but now a tiny neon green barrette fought to hold a bit of it back. Her brown eyes scanned the room as she stood there.

Patting Peanut Butter on the head, Kit said, "Hey, Peanut Butter."

Leanne quickly put Peanut Butter down and slammed into Kit with a hug. Almost falling backward for the second time, Kit was forced to lean in.

Not letting go, Kit pushed her back. "Can you do me a favor, Leanne?"

Leanne looked up and nodded.

"Can you make sure you don't put Peanut Butter in your bag?" Kit winked. "I wouldn't want Marjorie to hiss at you again."

"I-I won't, but P-Peanut B-b-Butter gets- scar-ed."

Kit watched Peanut Butter spiral around Leanne's legs. "I know. Peanut Butter is lucky to have you," she said.

Leanne walked away, back over to her spot near the cat tree in the far corner of the room. Something about her innocence reminded Kit of her childhood. She shrugged it off.

In the Cat Collectibles shop, a crowd of people was paying for tickets. A lunchtime crowd in need of cat love. She smiled, thinking she should get some too.

Swooping up a cat who walked by, she stuck her face in the fur and inhaled.

Ahh... how I have missed this. She held the cat while she looked around the room. The cushions on the bench were salmon colored, contrasting nicely with the hard-wood floor. Leanne was at the far end. A lady and her child sitting beside her were trying to coax a cat back to play. The cat was having none of it. Sadness flowed over the girl's face until an enormous cat rubbed her leg and plopped by her shoe, showing a massive belly. With a squeal of delight on both their faces, they gave the cat all the love they had.

There were tall windows and a floating cat perch positioned at every other window pane like macramé planters for cats—a Nan touch for sure. One calico cat had his head over the edge as he pawed anyone who walked by.

Another cat walked with ease around the wavy catwalk, jumping over to the box that Sarah mentioned needed fixing, its tail held high. A good place to get away from touchy people.

A few people were enjoying a snack or coffee as they watched the cats with delight. This place was so cozy.

Letting the cat drop to the floor, it landed on its feet, turned back, and blinked slowly.

Still nothing, Kit mused.

She returned to the parking lot to grab a bag and her suitcase.

Back inside, she paused at the office. Marjorie was on the phone, her hand waving a mile a minute. Kit could see a bright pink Post-it note that had the word "LITTER" in big black letters.

When Marjorie saw Kit at the door, she stopped talking and turned her chair in the opposite direction.

I don't want to look at you, either. As she adjusted the direction of her suitcase, Kit continued down the hall, noticing a door past the kitchen and another next to the office. She turned on the light to the room beside the office. The break room had high-top tables, probably left over from the old days, along with a microwave and a chalkboard.

Kit passed a tuxedo cat on a mission. A small cat with big eyes, tiny paws, and a pink collar, she moved fast, causing her collar charm to tinkle.

As the cat passed her, Kit heard mumbling.

She stopped short and stared at the cat.

"Crap, here we go." She shrugged and moved past the back door. Beyond this door was a large window that looked out onto a patio and a second parking lot. It was right across from her apartment door.

She noticed a girl with a green smock having lunch at a picnic table while texting on her phone.

This place looked so different from before. The parking lot wasn't as big as she remembered. She turned the key in the apartment door as a flood of memories hit her hard. She thought back to when her grandmother bought the place.

"It will be perfect here," she remembered her grandmother saying. "I'll have the café to keep me busy while you both go to college. What more do I need?"

Kit inhaled as she opened the door. Smaller than she remembered, but perfect.

The decor was a colorful mixture of bright colors with an ocean vibe. The perfect marriage between the seventies and boho. And that view of the ocean on the opposite side of the room was amazing. The sun bouncing off the waves was the therapy Kit needed.

Nan had made every area of this apartment feel like an oasis. The reading nook in the corner, the little seaside patio with the clematis blocking the sitting area from the café patrons. Even the little makeshift office near the front door was perfect.

Kit dropped her bag and moved through the open living room to the small kitchen. She wondered if she needed her own furniture now. Everything here was in better shape than her stuff in storage.

Kit drank a glass of water, then plopped on the couch. She grabbed a pillow and sniffed. *Smells like Nan and the ocean.*

"How I missed this," she said out loud. Exhaustion waved over her, but the need to run was stronger.

She jumped up quickly and rolled her suitcase into the bedroom.

After changing into a halter top, leggings, and running shoes, she stood on the front porch putting her earbuds in. She wondered how long it had been since she'd run down this coast.

Had to be right before I moved. A little over seven years ago. It just revealed how time could fly by yet somehow stay the same.

"Hope Grandma is enjoying her cruise," she whispered as she walked down the embankment and took off on the path at a slow pace.

CHAPTER 4

Morning came quickly. Kit wiped the sleep out of her eyes, then went to the kitchen to make coffee. Grabbing her favorite mug Nan had made for her during her college years, she added sugar, then went to take a shower.

Half an hour later, with her hair up in a towel, wearing her pink bathrobe and slippers, she returned to the coffeepot. From her window, she could see a sliver of the sun coming up.

Taking a chug of her coffee, she went to the bedroom and dressed in a sundress and flats. She wanted to take a few minutes alone in the café before everyone showed up. She opened the apartment door, looking down to make sure she had her café keys. Coffee still in hand, she stepped forward, but plowed into something hard, bending her wrist back as her fingers jammed into the coffee mug handle. Hot liquid splashed everywhere, including over her hand and dress.

"Ow!" Pain shot through her hand.

She stepped back. Her pocketbook dropped the same moment her mug hit the floor and shattered. Managing to keep her balance, she pulled off her wet dress, left it on the floor, and dashed in her underwear to the kitchen sink. The cold water felt good on her hand despite the throb in her fingers and wrist. She leaned over the sink, watching her hand turn red.

Glancing over her shoulder, she could see a silhouette of something large in the hallway blocking her door. Squinting, she made out large boxes piled high.

She kicked off her shoes and felt a throb in her big toe. Her anger rose, but the woozy feeling from the pain took over.

Just as she was ready to begin yelling, she noticed her mug on the floor in three pieces.

The anger was now mixed with a tinge of sorrow. "That was my favorite cup."

She turned the faucet off. Luckily, she had gone shopping the night before and, in the refrigerator, found a pack of frozen peas to use as an ice pack. She grabbed it and slammed the fridge door before hobbling to the bedroom. This time, she put on a red dress and brown open-toed shoes. Her toe was feeling better, but her hand was another story.

Standing in front of the open apartment door, she turned the light on to see fourteen boxes of cat litter on a pallet. Slamming her door shut, she screamed.

"Marjorie!"

Kit picked up the pieces of the mug and her wet dress. Her eyes welled up. Taking a deep breath in, she dropped the pieces of the mug into the sink. She got a towel for the spill. The memories of that mug spiraled her back to being a kid, hanging with Nan and drinking English tea. Well, not exactly English, as hers was half tea and half milk.

Kit left through the back door, and walked around the building, taking it all in as she tried to ignore her hand throbbing. She used her key to enter, and they jumped off their perches to greet her. A warm body rubbed against her leg.

"Good morning to you too, Daisy."

Daisy purred.

"You are adorable, but I can't feed you, my friend."

Daisy pulled Kit's injured hand over with a paw and sniffed.

"I'll be okay, little one." Daisy looked up. "You go along and play."

As if the cat understood, she wobbled over to a small tuxedo cat, the same one Kit had seen in the hall yesterday.

"At least you guys won't sabotage my job. I hope."

In the kitchen, she grabbed the peas again and winced as she placed the packet on her right hand.

The back door unlocked, and a tall woman with brown hair entered. She started when she saw Kit.

"Hey," she said. "I'm not used to anyone getting here so early."

"I'm not used to getting up this early," Kit said with half a smile.

The thin woman reached out her hand to shake. "I'm Janice Jordan. I'm the lead cook, or should I say, baker."

Putting her iced hand up. "I'm Kit. Sorry, I can't shake today."

"What happened?" Janice asked, adjusting her glasses.

"Honestly, I'm not sure. I'm going to head to the walk-in clinic, but I'll be back for the meeting this morning."

"I'll be ready," she said as she twisted her keys around her finger, heading for the kitchen. A light went on at the same time music started.

Kit walked in the front door as a fluffy white cat ran past her, chasing a beam of light from the window. Her hand bandaged and in pain, she felt ridiculous having to deal with this now. *I'm gonna punch the person in the nose who did this to me*, she thought, as she chuckled at the image of two bandaged hands.

Janice peeked her head out of the kitchen door.

"How did it go, Kit?"

She held up her half-bandaged hand. "I have a cracked bone in my wrist, sprained fingers, and second-degree burns."

"Damn. They didn't splint it?"

"They can't. I have a burn, so I need to watch it."

Kit sat down on a high-top chair in front of the office. Janice walked over and leaned in as she pushed her glasses up on her thin nose. "That looks uncomfortable," Janice said as she winced.

"Yeah, it smarts."

"Sorry you got hurt, but it is nice to have another manager around. Feels weird here without Nan."

"I bet. She's a force, for sure. Have you been here a while?" Kit asked.

Janice waved at a cat handler as she continued on. "I started after the cats came along. It's a nice place to work. I moved from Connecticut to get my baking degree in Providence. I loved Rhode Island, but I like the small town. It's more my speed. I started working here, and I haven't looked back."

"Yeah, this is a charming town." Kit smiled, despite a wave of pain that grabbed her attention.

"I got to get back to work." Janice nodded to Sarah as she walked back into the kitchen.

Sarah walked up. "I heard you got hurt. What happened?"

Kit was sharing the story but interrupted herself in the middle as she noticed Leanne's purple hair. "Did Leanne change her hair?"

Sarah leaned in to not be heard. "She changes it every few days. I think that's why it always looks matted. Some of the staff joke they can base their day by her hair color. Is it going to be a blue day or a pink day?"

"Well, a purple day's not bad," Kit said.

A black and brown tabby did his best to squish through the cat door on the opposite side of the room. Almost giggling, he plopped on his side, his brown collar clunking as he landed, and began washing his paws.

"Damn, that is a belly. Looks like he needs a bigger door and a diet," Kit said.

A cat handler walked by. "Hey, what's the name of that chunky cat?" Kit pointed in its direction.

"Oh, that's Trunk. He's probably the weirdest cat we got."

"How so?"

"He puts his paw in everything—coffee, water, you name it. And he licks walls."

Kit laughed. "Really?"

"Yup, must taste good," the cat handler said.

"They must. Who would have known walls are a savory delight." She watched Trunk enjoy his bath. Then still with his tongue sticking out, he looked up, distracted by a few meows from another cat in the cat box attached to the catwalk.

CHAPTER 5

K it decided to leave the café for a run to clear her mind. She changed as fast as she could and headed to the path. Running was her stress relief.

Kit ran as fast and far as she could to outrun anything that messed with her peace of mind.

Ponytail swinging back and forth, she wiped the sweat from her forehead and eyes with her sleeve. She kicked up the speed.

She focused her attention on the run, the rhythmic pounding of her shoes hitting the pavement. She followed a path lined with trees and low shrubs that filtered the sun as the breeze cooled her skin under her sweaty top. She waved her wrapped hand to another runner as he went by.

A thought crept into her mind. She couldn't shake the situation with Marjorie. She even wondered why Nan put up with her. It wasn't like her to tolerate fools.

Feeling a buzz in her pocket, she slowed down her jog and shoved her hand in the pocket, only to find a quick reminder of her injury.

"Ouch," she said, jumping a bit. She twisted to pull her pants toward the left to grab the phone with her good hand.

"Shit," she screamed. The phone flew out of her hand.

"Y...es," she finally answered the call between gasps.

"Kit, are you okay?" her grandmother said.

"Yes. Deep breathing. I went for a run and dropped my phone." Kit coughed. "Speak of the devil, I was just thinking about you."

"Okay, dear." Her grandmother's accent was strong today. "I don't know about any devil, but I will tell you I'm having a hell of a time! Did you make it to the café? Everything okay?"

"You forgot to mention a few important things, Nan," Kit breathed out as she finally caught her breath.

"Did I?"

Kit chugged her water. "Yes, you did. I pictured a tiny café with three cats and a barista named Sarah. Not fifteen cats and hundreds of employees."

"You're being silly, Kitty. There are not hundreds of employees. Pish."

"Well, it seems like it. The other thing you forgot to mention is your asshole manager."

"Marjorie? She's not bad. She can be rough around the edges, but she has a good heart."

"A good-hearted woman wouldn't have tried to sabotage my job on the first day. She broke my hand."

"I can't believe that," Nan said.

"I'm gonna send you the medical bill."

"Wait, you're serious?"

"Yes, Nan. I have a chipped bone in my wrist, sprained fingers, a burned hand, and your manager is behind it."

"Did you punch her?"

"Wait. No, I didn't, but that's a good idea."

"Oh, bugger. Kit, I got to go. I have to go get my dancing shoes. I'll call you in a few days. Be good, my dear. Loves you," she said, and the phone went dead.

Kit looked down at her phone. "Why can't this family just say goodbye like everyone else?" She shook her head.

The salty air hit her senses as she pivoted to head back home. The realization that she was gonna run the café on her own caused a wave of nausea. She also remembered the staff meeting was in an hour. She picked up speed.

CHAPTER 6

Trunk squished into the cat box and sat down.

"Ouch, will you get your fat ass off my tail!" Gabby howled. She put her tiny paw out and popped Trunk a few times on the nose.

He closed his eyes, recoiling, but only long enough to adjust his position. He moved toward the front of the wooden box they shared. Their box was connected to a walkway mounted high on the wall in the Feline Foyer.

Shifting her weight to the opposite side, Gabby tried to get to the front.

"Come on, Trunk. I can't see beyond your fat butt. Can you move it over? You're squishing me."

Trunk leaned to the right.

"Ah, thank you." Gabby hung her paw out of the box, focusing her eyes downward.

"This is not just your box, Gabby. You need to share," Trunk said as he slid in beside her.

Gabby blinked. At another box, she saw Daisy sitting with her paws crossed.

"Hi, Gabby," said Daisy as she licked her white paw. "Hey, Trunk."

Gabby and Trunk nodded a greeting.

Daisy laid her head on her front paws and looked down. "What's going on down there?"

"A meeting," Gabby said. She turned to Trunk, who had turned around again. "You take up the entire space, and you're not even facing the right direction. Ouch! You're still on my tail!" Gabby hissed.

"Oh," Trunk murmured, lifting his butt. Gabby pulled her tail free, meowed, and stepped on Trunk. She jumped through the hole above and sat on top of the box.

Trunk's tabby face appeared in the hole, his green eyes narrowed. "You didn't need to step on me."

Looking back at Trunk, Gabby wiggled her whiskers. Her tiny frame had taken up half the diameter of the hole, but Trunk's face filled it. If a cat could laugh, she would do it right then.

Trunk flopped to his side and stretched out, still facing the wrong direction. He turned back around and flopped again. He pressed his massive paws against the inside of the box.

Trunk meowed, which caused Gabby to stick her head back through the hole. Her round, dark eyes peered in. "Will you be quiet? I am trying to hear this."

Gabby returned her attention to the group below. She noticed the new woman put a finger over her lips.

"Is she shushing me?" Although a cat, Gabby would have none of it.

Trunk, now asleep, snored.

"Oh, for the love of catnip, you got to be kidding." Gabby leaped off the box and walked over to Daisy.

She jumped into Daisy's box.

"You are welcome here, but don't put your feet on my fur," Daisy said.

Gabby eased her front paw closer to Daisy. Daisy looked down at it and back up at Gabby. Gabby tucked it under her chest.

Daisy liked Gabby. She was fun, especially since the incident with Mr. Buttons, her good friend.

"Six feet away, and he's still loud!" Gabby cocked an ear in Trunk's direction. "They should call him Truck, not Trunk. He sounds like a truck backfiring."

Daisy expressed a soft whirl.

Distracted by noises below, they turned their focus back to the humans' meeting. "The one who is talking, I don't like her. She is a grouch, and she is mean," Daisy said.

"I like the one with the bandaged paw. She is sassy."

"She patted my head today. I feel bad about her hurt paw. She had on a pretty dress today. This outfit she's wearing now, not so nice," Daisy said, blinking.

"That dress didn't match her red hair," Gabby said.

Daisy looked over at Gabby. "When did you start to care about clothes?"

"You started it."

"Well, she would look better in blue. Would match her blue eyes."

"She needs to eat a burger. She is skinny."

Daisy tsked. "Gabby, maybe *you* need to stop eating treats; you're getting paunchy too."

"You're just jealous. I have thicker fur than you do. It makes me look fluffy."

Daisy smiled. "If you say so."

Gabby stretched her paw out and yawned. "That woman feels familiar, and she kept an eye on Peanut Butter when he was afraid of that lady. Maybe she'll stay."

"She upset the mean one. My kind of human. Hey, what's Vee doing down there?" Daisy asked.

"Looking for a feather or using that kid's legs as a scratching post. That kid is covered in her fur." Gabby giggled.

Daisy and Gabby continued to watch as they listened to the rhythmic snoring of Trunk, which soon lulled them into doing the same.

CHAPTER 7

Kit entered the Feline Foyer only to get bombarded by that annoying voice. Marjorie. Her voice was five octaves too high and nasal. Kit wondered if it would put a cat in heat.

Kit walked over, wiping sweat off her brow with her towel. "How come every time I walk into this café, I hear you yelling?"

Marjorie smirked and glanced down at Kit's hand, then looked behind her at the staff.

Fourteen staff members had shown up, gathered in the corner, and giving the cats pets and cuddles. A few felines sat high in their boxes, watching and judging.

Kit slid over to Brian, who was squished on the couch by a few young baristas. *Who can blame them?* Kit thought.

He smiled, which made him look like a Viking. No one would want to run into him at night. Luckily, he was a gentle giant.

Kit looked at the cats in the boxes above and gave them a *shh* since they were louder than the staff. "Do they always get this loud during a meeting?"

Brian laughed, his broad shoulders moving up and down. "Yup, I think they think they're part of it, which they are, in a way. It's all about them, especially Gabby, the tuxedo in the middle. She loves to be number one and she'll get it by force if necessary. She's in charge."

"She's so little."

"Don't let her size fool you. She keeps them all in check. Even Trunk."

"Way to go, girl," Kit said with a smile.

Kit's palms were sweating as her focus narrowed. Today she was grateful that all thirty staff members hadn't shown up. Fourteen was enough.

She ran her speech through her mind one more time before starting.

"Hi, everyone. I don't know you all yet, but over the next few weeks, I will do my best to learn all your names. Even the cat names," she said, scanning the furry faces.

"I'm Kit Beck. Nan is my grandmother, and if you haven't heard, she's off on a cruise."

"Is she coming back?" a girl from the back shouted.

"Yes, but I don't know when. She is enjoying herself on a cruise. And if you know her, she'll be the life of the party. She left Marjorie in charge, but I'll be seeing to the day-to-day operations and oversight." Kit looked over at Marjorie, who puffed up. "I'm not here to change any-thing—yet."

Marjorie turned her head away.

Kit continued. "I *am* gonna see what we can improve, but for now, the most important thing is to continue to keep the cats safe and our patrons happy."

She paused for effect. "Two things I will not tolerate. Cruelty to animals or games. I also want you to enjoy your job and have fun. But remember, this is a business."

Kit looked over to see Janice in the corner next to Sarah. Janice, about eight inches taller, was staring at the floor. Sarah, her blonde hair pulled back into a twist, stood there with her arms crossed, a scowl on her face, as she eyed a few employees in the back who weren't paying attention. Sarah cleared her throat, and the room went quiet.

Kit continued to tell them her expectations. As always, an audience, especially a small one like her previous job, helped her nerves settle after a few moments.

"One more thing." She held up her bandaged hand.

"*This* is what I call games. I have a broken hand, sprained fingers, and a burned wrist. I will not tolerate this. I've been here for less than twenty-four hours, and someone thought it would be fun to put a crate of litter boxes in front of my apartment door."

Kit heard mumbling and saw a sea of concerned faces. "Someone was told to put them there, and that person had to be strong."

Brian said something, but Kit's attention faded for a moment. In her mind...*Marjorie fell to the floor, and because of her T-rex hands, she couldn't get back up. Watching her thrash around was exhilarating. Kit held up her bandaged wrist. Sorry, can't help ya.*

Kit shook herself back to reality. She noticed Marjorie leaving the room.

"I am not finished, Marjorie," Kit spoke up as she put her good hand on her hip.

Marjorie sat back down. Someone snickered from the back of the room.

"Anyone have anything they would like to add?" Kit looked around as the noise level in the room began to rise.

Marjorie stood again, and Kit felt her muscles tighten.

Keep it cool.

The manager clasped her tiny hands together and looked like she was addressing a church congregation. Everyone quieted down again.

Vee, the calico cat, walked around everyone's legs leaving fur on the unexpected. She purred and got a few pets from a kid in the back.

"We need to work on our budget. We should revoke a few free passes that were given years ago." She placed a hand on her chest and attempted what Kit assumed was a sad, puppy dog face. "I love Nan, but she is not all that business savvy. We have a dozen people who come and go as they please, not paying the hourly rate that the rest of our patrons pay, and they hang out here all day long."

Sarah spoke up. "Those people helped Nan before the café was full of cats. That was her gift to them."

"My mom was one of her first customers to visit the cats. She gets a discount every year. I think it's nice of Nan to do that," a barista from the back said.

Marjorie said in a dismissive tone, "Yes, but that was years ago." She rolled her eyes and continued. "How long are we going to give away things for free? Some abuse it."

"My mother *never* abused it," the barista said.

"Okay, Marjorie. Thanks for bringing that up. I'll look at it," Kit said.

"Well, I think we should talk more about it. We should have a vote." Marjorie smiled, and the staff followed suit.

Oh no, she didn't. She narrowed her eyes at Marjorie, feeling the red in her cheeks.

"The budget is not a group discussion."

"If we could give everyone a raise, it would be," Marjorie suggested as she tipped her head and smiled sweetly at Kit. The talking and now cheers got louder.

Kit raised her voice over the din in the room. "I will look into everything we've discussed. I appreciate you coming. We will meet next month. The meeting dates will be in the newsletter."

"What newsletter?" Brian said.

"The newsletter you'll be getting. Check your email, and if you don't have an email account, let Marjorie know. She'll help you set one up," Kit announced. Marjorie frowned.

From the back of the room, a brown-haired kid shouted. "Are we getting a raise?"

Kit walked over to the kid, recognizing him. He shifted his weight. "Peter, right?"

The kid now rocked back and forth. "Um, yeah."

Kit raised her right arm. "Did you do this, Peter?"

He looked at Marjorie and back at Kit. "No. I would ne–"

"Well, Peter, that's good. As for the raise, I'll get back to you on it. It's my first week, and I haven't looked at the budget. Okay?"

"Oh, yeah. Fine," he said. He nodded his head, and his bangs fell over his right eye.

As everyone left, Kit whispered in Marjorie's ear, "Marjorie, a word in the office."

Kit shut the door behind them.

Marjorie jumped right in.

"The meeting went well, huh?"

"What the hell was that?" Kit snapped.

"I don't understand," Marjorie said with a big smile.

"Knock it off, Marjorie!" She put her left hand on her hip. "When has a budget meeting ever been a vote with employees? That was out of line!"

Marjorie just stared.

Kit leaned over the boxes on the couch to lower the venetian blinds and her voice.

"Your only goal is to get rid of Leanne. It will not work."

Marjorie inspected her nails. "Well, I figured, being a businesswoman and all, you would see the benefit of a good business decision."

This time Kit said nothing, just stared into Marjorie's beady eyes.

She raised her bandaged hand. "Monday. We are having a long talk."

Marjorie looked at her hand, then made eye contact.

"Good. We can discuss the raise," she said, then bolted out of the office.

As the door closed, Kit grabbed a pillow from the couch and screamed into it. There was a sudden silence in the café. She opened the door and stuck her head out. Everyone was staring in her direction.

"Sorry, stubbed my toe!" she said with a half smile, closing the door.

She slumped down in a corner of the couch. A tear fell from her eye.

Kit had been crying for a few moments when she heard a scratch on the door.

She opened it to find Gabby, who quickly slid in.

"Another crying human. Suppose I should rub against her so she can cry all over my fur."

Kit laughed. "I won't mess up your fur. You're sweet, though."

Gabby froze, her eyes wide open. "Did she understand me?"

Kit smiled.

Gabby looked sideways. "Nah, it's my imagination."

"Your imagination is good, then. Yes, I understand you," Kit said between sniffles.

Gabby jumped back as if someone had tossed a toy at her. "Whoa! This is freaky."

This small tuxedo cat sat still, tipping her dainty head to the left.

"You saw the meeting, huh?" Kit asked.

"I've seen worse. Figured the mean one might try to punch you, and since you're already injured... I saw what was going on in here too. I love a good catfight," Gabby said.

Kit grinned.

"Can you hear the other cats?" Gabby asked.

Kit began twirling her hair. "Well, it's weird. I can only hear parts of what they say. Daisy doesn't seem to speak."

"She actually talks a lot. But you're not missing much—a bunch of crap about her fur. Nothing important."

"Gabby!"

"We didn't get along at one time. She was snooty. It's better now, but she's only interested in how cute she looks. And you better run if you get something on her fur. Well, I gotta go!"

Kit raised her hands up. "Hey, what happened to comforting the crying human?"

"You're not crying anymore, and besides, I can talk to you later," Gabby said as she padded out the door.

CHAPTER 8

K it walked out of the Feline Foyer and into the parking lot.

Brian jogged up to her. "Kit? I'm not sure how those boxes got there, but I'll find out."

Kit paused by her car. "She told someone to do it. She doesn't have a good poker face." She rubbed her sore hand.

"We'll move them."

"Thanks," Kit said, realizing why Sarah liked him.

"Marjorie feeds off people. She likes to see people squirm," he said.

Kit and Brian chatted for a few minutes before she finally got in the car. Safe inside, tears filled her eyes. Her hands shook.

Damn it! She fought with the seat belt.

Frustrated, she slammed her hand into the car panel. She wiped her eyes and called Tess on speakerphone before pulling out of the lot.

"Kit! Oh my god, I've been waiting to talk to you. I thought about you all day. Sorry I didn't get back to you. It's been foreva, gurl." Tess's Southern drawl sounded more fake than real.

Kit gasped between tears.

"Kit, what's wrong, sugar?" Tess asked.

"I don't think I should have moved. This is so hard. I'm back home–."

Tess squealed. "I'm so excited you're here, even if you're not. What's going on?"

"I'm taking over the cat café for Nan." Kit paused. "I've failed already."

Tess lowered her voice. "Aww, sweetie. You're probably doing great. You always think the worst. You put too much pressure on yourself."

Kit told her the story of her broken hand, the litter boxes, and of course, Marjorie.

"Eww. I've met Marjorie. She's about as delightful as road-kill."

"How do you—"

"I worked with that nightmare about five years ago. Nan needed help to get the cats settled. Marjorie manipulated everyone except your grandmother. She never played her games with her. But with us, she was so bitchy and vindictive. Can't trust a woman with beady eyes," Tess said.

Kit rolled her eyes. "I know. It took her one day to get me. I don't understand how Nan couldn't see this." Kit's phone beeped.

"Hold on, Tess."

Kit answered the other line. "Yes, this is Kitty, but I prefer Kit."

She heard a woman with a soft voice. "This is Brenda from Converse Counseling. I have paperwork for your anger management—"

"Yeah, not a good time," Kit said.

"I won't take up much of it. We need to make an appointment for this week," Brenda said.

"Yeah, I'll call you later." Kit hung up.

"Who was that?" Tess asked.

"The counselor for that stupid anger management therapy."

"Kit, you can't ignore that. It's mandatory. As in, get your ass to the session."

"I can't deal with that right now. I'm just overwhelmed. This is too much for me. I just want to go sit on my couch, binge on popcorn, and watch a movie."

Tess sighed. "Fine, take an evening and do that, but don't stay on the couch for too long. You were *becoming* the couch in California."

Kit smiled but said nothing.

"Do me a favor, Kit. Trust your intuition. It is so strong. Not to change the subject, but how's it going with the cats?"

"I've only heard one, so far. A little tuxedo. She has a big personality for a tiny body."

"It's time, Kit. Embrace your gifts," Tess said.

"You might be right about this one thing. But I can't deal with that either right now. It's been a bad day."

"Listen, I got to go. Kit, don't let Marjorie get to you. Bullies are weak, remember that. Besides, your bestie is here, and I'll kick her ass if you need me to."

Kit chuckled. "I bet you can."

"You know it! I'll call you tomorrow. We need to get a few drinks. Bye, gurl." Tess hung up.

Kit pulled into the parking lot of the liquor store, turned the car off, and leaned her head back.

A buzzing feeling coursed through her body. She shivered. This was the same feeling she'd had on the run. She wondered, *Am I missing California?* The warehouse job sucked, but she knew what they expected of her. She pulled the visor down to adjust her hair and check her makeup in the mirror. As she stepped out of the car, that feeling lingered. *Something is wrong.* Ignoring the thought, she walked into the liquor store.

CHAPTER 9

L ike Trunk, Kit plopped on the couch, feeling excited, exhausted, and a little drunk.

What a surprise. Tess had picked Kit up early in the evening. They went out, had a few drinks, and talked about everything. Kit found her nerves were more settled. Then Tess insisted they go back to the cat café to see the apartment. Instead, she was led to the break room for a surprise party to welcome her to the café. The staff was great, and the cake was to die for. Luckily she never saw Marjorie.

I should have grabbed another piece of cake.

Her ability to sit upright was quickly waning. She thought she heard a scratch on the door.

"Oh no, more boxes." She giggled and tipped over on the couch.

She sat upright again. "Wine! I left my wine on the sideboard. Maybe I'll grab some more cake too."

She emptied her purse out on the kitchen table, looking for the keys that she eventually found in her pocket. She laughed as she opened the door to find Daisy.

"What are you doing here?" Kit struggled to pronounce each word.

Daisy walked down the hall, looking back occasionally.

Kit walked toward the Feline Foyer.

Bump. Bump.

Kit stopped short, almost tripping herself.

"What the hell is that?"

Bump. Bump.

She leaned against the wall and tried to tune in to the noise. Daisy meowed by the break room as Kit pushed herself off the wall. Standing in the middle of the hall, she noticed the wine bottle on the side table. Tiptoeing past the break room, she grabbed the wine bottle by the neck, tipping it upside down like a hammer, and raised it as she turned back toward the break room door.

Bump. Bump.

Then a muffled *Meow!*

She lowered the wine bottle and sighed in relief.

She opened the door. "Who shut this door on you?" she asked, looking down at Trunk, just visible in the hall light.

Daisy walked in the room, sniffed, and turned around. Her job done, she padded away.

Kit looked back at Trunk in the doorway.

"What are you covered in?" She switched the light on.

"Aww, no! The cake!"

It looked half-eaten and was covered in cat prints. "Did you eat the cake, Trunk?"

Trunk just shook his head and blinked.

"What is on you? That's not cake frosting."

As she walked toward the cake, she jumped back. She noticed a large lump on the floor.

"What!"

In front of her, slumped over, was Marjorie. The cake knife stuck straight in her back.

Gabby sat on Marjorie's back, paw-popping the knife handle. With every hit of her paw, the knife wobbled and slammed into the table leg.

Bump. Bump.

If Marjorie wasn't dead, she'd have yelled at the cat to get off her back. Literally.

"Gabby, get off her back. That is not a toy! No, please don't lick the knife—"

Kit, barely keeping her balance, leaned down and moved closer. It seemed Trunk and Gabby had been there a while. Blood- and frosting-covered paw prints encircled Marjorie.

"Well, there goes my cake." Kit sighed. She struggled with the wine bottle's screw top, using her left hand. Finally, she took a few gulps of wine.

"Hmm. Not bad."

She slowly stood up, careful not to tip over, and closed the door to keep the cats in. She walked to the back of the room and put the wine down.

As curious as a cat, she carefully observed everything.

The cats looked like Carrie from the Stephen King novel. Blood dripped off their collars and ears. Marjorie looked dead.

Kit didn't feel happy or sad. This lady was a nightmare, just like this scene.

"At least she's quiet for a change," Kit said out loud.

The pool of blood by her side was very dark. Kit could see purple blotches on her face. She'd been there a while.

Kit stared, unable to look away. She noticed the knife. It matched the knife that was left with the cake early on. On the table was a cash register drawer that had money in it, splattered with frosting and a bit of blood.

Kit squatted to look directly at Marjorie's face. Her eyes were open in a dead stare. Kit realized she wouldn't win this staring match.

She stood up, walking in a pattern around the blood. Not realizing her hands were shaking, she grabbed the wine bottle, took a few more gulps, and went back to her apartment to get her phone.

Before she called the police, she took some pictures. *Priorities*, she thought.

Kit stood in the middle of the Feline Foyer and dialed 911. *Two days on the job, and there's a murder. Damn.*

"Yes, I want to report a murder. I'm at the Caddy Cat Café." She rolled her eyes. "No, it's not a cat. It's a human."

Kit punched the numbers on the keypad so the cops could enter, then she sat down on the bench near the door. She looked down at her hands, still trembling. She fought through the tremors to move the pictures from her phone to the cloud.

Kit suddenly realized there was a murderer in the café. Her eyes went wide, and her thoughts raced. She took another few gulps from the bottle.

CHAPTER 10

"Your name is?"

"Kit Beck."

"Is that your real name?" the detective asked.

"Kitty."

He smirked and scribbled in his book. "You work here?" He handed a piece of paper to his deputy.

"You found the body?" he asked.

"Yes, in the break room. Be careful when you open the door. There are two cats in there having a party."

"You left them in there?"

"Yup. They were playing with the knife. Figured they might be evidence."

Kit kept her head down. Alcohol and stress usually made her laugh. She was terrified it might happen any minute.

"What is the victim's name?"

"Marjorie Pigeon. Pigeon as in bird."

"How long ago did you find her?"

"About ten minutes. Give or take. There was a welcome party for me in the break room. I wanted another piece of cake and my wine bottle that I left on that table over there."

"You drove from your house to get wine?"

"No. My apartment is down the hall. My grandmother owns this place. I'm taking over while she's off on a cruise."

Kit noticed the detective was handsome in an older sort of way. He was deliberate and to the point. He looked down at his notes. "Who is Marjorie?"

"Manager and not a very good one. I'll be honest; she was going to be fired next week."

He looked up at Kit.

"She had a few problems with employees, including me." Kit held up her bandaged hand.

"She did that to you?"

"Not exactly. But she had someone block my apartment door with a pallet of cat litter. I fractured and burned my hand slamming into the boxes holding a coffee cup."

"Did you kill her?" the detective asked.

"Seriously?" She held up her bandaged hand again, showing the burn and bruise on her fingers.

He pointed his pen at her hand. "Good alibi."

The deputy, a young man in his twenties, reappeared, looked at Kit, then handed the detective a form. The younger officer whispered in his ear and walked away.

"Kitty, I'm looking at your file. You seem to have a history of outbursts. Care to explain?"

"Yup, people irritate me. And call me Kit, please."

"Okay. Can you elaborate a bit?"

Kit adjusted her weight on the bench.

"I was jogging. Two old people were skating. They got in my way, so I gave them a little push." Kit looked down.

"They didn't use their brakes, and the old man got hurt." She looked out at the Feline Foyer. "I did an oops." She took a gulp of her bottle, then exhaled loudly. "They didn't press charges, but the judge wants me to see a counselor for my anger issues. End of story."

"There is more to that story."

"Yup. But I'm not sharing." Kit waved her arm. "Do your detective work and figure it out yourself." Kit grabbed her bottle and took another gulp. She looked around and realized the place was now filled with cops and people in white suits. It was busier than a Saturday afternoon.

"Okay. Try not to drink so much. I may have more questions."

"Detective, what is your name?"

He turned back around. "Detective Kale Flowers."

"Kale, as in seaweed?" Kit asked with a grin.

He smiled and walked toward the break room.

"Don't drink, he said. Right." She talked to herself, pacing back and forth for what felt like hours.

The detective walked over, shaking his head. "You're still drinking, I see. Who was working tonight?"

Kit leaned back for balance. "Um, I need to go to that office to check." She pointed in the wrong direction.

He grabbed for the bottle, but she pulled back her hand. "I think we have had enough."

"I dis...agree, but whatever."

Kit zigzagged to the office, snapped the schedule off the wall, sending everything else fluttering to the ground. "Brian. He wrangles the kitties." She laughed hard. "I mean, he handles. Handles the kitties. He's the cat handler, not a wrangler. Janice, she cooks."

"Does she cook the kitties?" Detective Flowers asked.

She tipped her head to the side. "You're funny."

"What are the names of the cats that you left in the room?"

"The tiny bloody one is Gabby, and the frosted one is Trunk."

"You think they killed her?"

"I wouldn't be surprised." She put the bottle on the desk and fell back on the office couch. "If you need help solving the murder, let me know." Pushing stuff off the cushions and onto the floor, she reached up and pulled the blanket down on top of her.

"What are you doing?"

"Taking a catnap. Murder investigations are exhausting. If you could find me a cat out there, I'll sleep better. Just not one of the bloody ones."

The detective stood in the doorway, looking down at Kit.

"The bloody ones are coming with us for evidence removal," he said. "Before you pass out, can you tell me who would do this?"

"Nope."

"You just told me to ask you if I needed help solving the murder. That's all you got?"

She flipped the covers over her head. In a muffled voice, she said, "She was a bitch, so it could have been anyone."

The door slammed.

Kit jumped a bit but laid back down.

"Kit!" Sarah said.

Kit pulled the blanket off her head and dropped her head back on the couch.

"Ouch." She held her head.

Sarah's voice was now high. "Kit, come on, tell me what happened."

"I. Need. Coffee."

Sarah lifted the venetian blinds up an inch and peeked out the office window.

"I snuck in. I can't go out there. They have yellow tape around this place," Sarah said. "What happened?"

Kit rubbed her temples. She sat upright and turned to put her feet on the floor.

Still holding her head in her hands, she managed, "I found Marjorie dead. Someone murdered her."

Sarah exhaled. "Oh, thank god!"

Kit looked up at Sarah. "Not the reaction I expected."

"No, not that. I thought it might be Brian."

Sarah sat down next to Kit.

"Why would you think it was Brian?" Kit asked.

Sarah looked down at her phone. "He's not answering my calls."

Kit shook her head and leaned back on the couch, pulling her knees to her chest. "I can't believe this. A new job and a murder. I told her she was done. That we were having a talk on Monday."

"Kit, you meant the job, not done-done, as in murder."

"All the same in the cop world. I'm glad the cats didn't get hurt."

"What happened to her?" Sarah leaned back too.

"Someone stuck a knife in her back. They locked the cats in the room. Cake, frosting, and blood everywhere. That cake was tasty too. What a shame."

Sarah scrunched her nose. "Eww, really?"

Kit leaned toward Sarah and snickered. "You should have seen Gabby. She was hitting the knife with her paw. Looked like a game of ping-pong. She even had blood dripping from her ears. If it wasn't so tragic, I would have laughed."

Kit looked at Sarah with a big grin.

Sarah smiled. "You did laugh, didn't you?"

Kit covered her mouth, shoulders bouncing. "Of course. It was funny." She burst out laughing.

Sarah laughed. "You are so bad."

The door opened, and Detective Flowers walked in. He looked directly at Sarah. "And you are?"

Sarah gasped. "My name is Sarah, sir."

"You walked into my murder scene?"

Sarah put her hands up. "I didn't go anywhere near the break room. I walked directly to the office to make sure Kit and the cats were okay. I swear."

"Kit and the cats, huh? Sounds like a bad boy band. Say goodbye, Sarah. I want you out in five." He closed the door.

"He's delightful," Sarah said.

Kit put her head down on her knees, sniffing the blanket. "My head hurts. You got any Tylenol?"

"I think there's some in the top drawer." Sarah walked around a few boxes and started pulling things from the desk. She tossed a bottle of Tylenol at Kit, who grabbed the wine and chugged several pills down.

"Remind me to keep water bottles in here," she said with her mouth still full of wine and dribbling out.

Sarah gave a thumbs-up. Still browsing through the desk drawer, she pulled out a pink envelope and opened it.

"Kit, look at this."

"I can't see straight. What is it?" Kit said.

"Marjorie. She had a shit list."

Kit chuckled. "Am I on it?"

Sarah pointed back and forth between Kit and herself. "We're both on it!"

Kit tipped her bottle of wine at Sarah. "Well, cheers to that. I made someone's list. Who else is on it?"

Sarah snorts. "Her husband, her mother, Leanne, Brian—"

"Wait, who's not on it?" Kit asked.

Sarah scanned the list and looked up at Kit. "Your grandmother."

Kit took another sip of wine. "She's lucky because I would have had to kill her. She is, or was, a piece of work. Leave that on the desk. I'll give it to the detective."

Sarah stood there for a moment, looking at the list. "Who do you think did it?"

Kit shrugged. "I don't know. Let me see the list."

She leaned forward and put her feet back on the floor but dropped her phone. "Rats, my fingers aren't working. Can you take a few pictures of it?"

Sarah picked up Kit's phone, snapped a few pictures, then handed the phone back to Kit, who dropped the phone on the couch.

Sarah put the paper back in the envelope and left it on the laptop. "Are you going to be okay? I need to get going before I get arrested."

"Yeah, I'll stay here for a bit. He may have more questions. Besides, they're processing Gabby and Trunk."

Sarah opens her eyes wide. "Processing? What does that mean?"

"They have to take pictures and look at their fur. Maybe test it for blood, not sure. Then they'll need to be cleaned. That will be fun," she said, taking another sip of wine.

"Kit, you can't clean two cats who are covered in blood while drunk. It will look like another murder scene and Brian will have a fit if you mess up the PP Parlor."

"Frosting."

"What?"

"They're also covered in frosting."

"I'll keep trying to call Brian. Hopefully, he'll get back to me soon." Sarah looked back at her phone.

Kit squinted her eyes as she looked at the clock on the wall. "What time is it?"

"Eleven thirty."

"Damn. Well, you can't keep texting him. It's too late."

"Yes, I can. Those cats mean everything to him. I'm going to step out and talk to the staff; a few are in the parking lot, terrified. Small-town rumors are the shit. If you need me, text me." Sarah was at the door, ready to leave. "I'll let you know when I get hold of Brian. We'll take care of it. Won't be our first cat mess to clean. He'll come in."

"Yeah, but blood? Ick." Kit stuck her tongue out.

"I can't stand the smell of blood. Makes me gag." Sarah plugged her nose as she walked out.

Kit took the last sip of wine and surveyed the office. She closed one eye.

How can I make this room look better? she thought. *Get rid of all the boxes, paperwork, and clutter. Move the desk toward the back and put another one next to it. Light-colored curtains on the window that faces the Feline Foyer. A clean couch, plants that don't look dead, and maybe some paint. Something lighter than this dark green. The artwork has got to go too. It would be good to have Sarah here. She deserves a space to get away from everyone to do her paperwork.*

Kit rubbed her eyes.

"Jeez, Kit, Marjorie hasn't even been dead for half a day, and you're redecorating," she said out loud.

She stood up and fell back on the couch. Giggling, she tried to stand again. Balancing on her heels, she centered herself and straightened her hair.

"A mirror. We need a mirror in here."

She grabbed the pink envelope off the desk.

She grabbed the door for stability and cracked it open slightly. As she turned to look toward the right, the detective was standing right there. She jumped back against the door, almost falling over.

"Crap! You scared me."

"What are you doing lurking?"

She sighed. "I was actually coming out to find you. When will the cats be finished with processing?"

"Soon."

She handed him the envelope. "Helping you with the murder. Here. Marjorie had a shit list."

He raised an eyebrow. "Are you on it?"

She rolled her eyes. "Of course. Along with everyone else, including her mother."

He exhaled loudly. "Okay. I'm still going to fingerprint you."

She held up her bandaged hand. "How are you going to get around this?"

"The techs are good."

Detective Flowers stayed near the door. Mostly, he kept his head down but seemed to know exactly where everyone was. She wondered if he ever smiled or did anything other than smirk.

"You're not a suspect right now. Although by the angle of the knife, we can't yet tell if it was a right- or left-handed assailant."

Kit leaned in with excitement. "That's cool."

The detective stared at her.

"That came out wrong. I need to sit back down. I've had way too much to drink."

"How much have you drunk tonight?"

"I plead the Fifth," she said.

He nodded his head. "Yup, that's about right. A fifth too much."

"Hmmm. I see you're attempting humor again," Kit said.

She noticed a small grin on his face. "Can I leave?"

"As long as you're not driving, yes. You can leave after the fingerprinting. She'll come over and do that right here."

"I'm not driving. I just need to walk down that hallway to my apartment. I told you I live here."

"No," he said.

"You just said I could leave."

He made another note in his book. "Yes, you can, but you're not walking down that hall. You're not walking past the yellow tape."

Kit stepped out of the doorway and looked down the hall. There was yellow tape from the tall counter to the other wall. The investigative team walked under it, in and out of the break room. It was like a scene from CSI.

"Can I go around the building and into my apartment?"

"As soon as we're done, you can stagger back to your apartment," he said.

"That's nice of you. My other question is, who will take care of the cats?"

He stopped writing. "Cats?"

"You are in a cat café. What do you think we have, stuffed animals?"

He looked around. "I only saw two cats."

Kit looked at him and down at his notepad. "You should write this down. We have fifteen cats. All this probably freaked them out, so they hid, but the moment it calms down, they will roam around your crime scene."

"Oh," he said, scratching his chin with his pen. "I can post an officer to keep the cats from roaming."

"Are you sure they're up to it? Wrangling cats is difficult."

He puffed out his chest. "I think my officers can handle a few cats."

Kit grinned and closed the office door.

CHAPTER 11

The sun slammed into Kit's eyes as she rolled over in bed. Shielding them with her hand, she looked at the clock. Five forty a.m.

"Damn."

She looked at her fingers, which were all black.

For a moment, it startled her until she remembered being fingerprinted the night before. The memories of the evening and the murder rushed back. There was still a murderer on the loose, and she'd slept like a baby.

She reached out to grab her phone and pulled it under the covers. She dimmed the phone light and scrolled through her messages. Seven showed up, but only two were important. Sarah had reached Brian, and Nan called.

Kit threw off the covers and sat up in bed. Her head pounded like a jackhammer. As she leaned on the bed, she realized her hand hurt too. She slid off the bed and searched for her slippers. She put the wrong slipper on and kicked it across the room.

"Damn it!"

She moved over to the slipper and slid it back on as she meandered to the bathroom.

Still wearing her pajamas, she put a red hoodie on, pulled the hood over her head, and cinched the string tight. She walked to the dining room sliding door facing the ocean and opened it. She closed her eyes and breathed deeply. As she basked in the sun, she could feel the coolness of the ocean and the smell of the salty air. Peace for a moment, at least.

This situation was more than she could handle. A wave of nausea hit her hard. She ran into the bathroom and drank from the faucet until the feeling passed.

"I need to call Nan," she said to the sink.

Kit headed to the kitchen and put on the coffee. She grabbed her computer and took it to her dining room table. Standing there twirling her hair, she turned the laptop on. She closed her eyes and listened to the computer fan. After signing on to Zoom, she tipped the camera down and headed back to the kitchen.

"Good morning, Kit." She heard her grandmother's voice from across the room.

"Good morning, Nan. Let me get my coffee. Be right there."

Kit went back with her coffee and sat down.

"Can you see me?" Nan asked.

"Not yet," Kit said as she sipped her coffee.

On the computer, she saw movement and heard a thump as her grandmother's image appeared. Kit smiled.

Nan's face took up the entire screen. Her voice boomed. "It's good to see you, dear."

Kit winced. "Nan, back up a bit. All I can see is your enormous nose, and you're loud as hell."

Nan backed up. "We have the same nose, dear," she said. She took a sip of her tea.

"How is your vacation?"

"Oh Kitty, it's lovely here. We are getting it on well."

"Getting on what?"

"Fun, my dear, just fun. We'll be in Jamaica tomorrow and stay for four days."

"That's nice. Listen, I need to tell you something." Kit paused. "There has been a terrible accident. Someone killed Marjorie."

Nan leaned back in her chair. "What? How?"

Kit grabbed her head. "Not so loud, Nan."

Nan whispered. "What the bloody hell happened?"

"She was murdered by someone. It happened last night. I found her in the break room with a knife sticking out of her back. There have been cops here all night."

Nan put her hands to her face. "Oh, my goodness. Are you okay, my dear?"

"I don't know. I drank too much last night. My head and hand hurt, and it shot my nerves. But it could be worse. I could be dead."

"Don't say that, please."

An unsettled feeling took over. Kit sipped her coffee.

Nan pointed to Kit's hands. "I see they printed you. You didn't kill her, did you? I know your temp—"

Kit put her coffee down. "Of course not! I was too drunk to hold a knife, plus my right hand is useless. Besides, that cake was to die for, no pun intended. I wouldn't have ruined it."

"A cake?" Nan said.

"Never mind. I'll be honest, Nan. I'm not sad she's dead. She was nasty."

"Kitty, she is difficult, or should I say *was* difficult, but she had a kind heart."

"Are we talking about the same person? Your manager? The one that looked like a T-rex?"

"That's harsh. She had rough features, but T-rex, no. Well, she had short arms and—"

"Then you don't believe me?"

"I...well...Kitty, you get upset easily."

Kit felt her eyesight narrow. *Her bandaged hand reached through the computer to wrap around Nan's neck. Just before it touched her skin, she pulled it back.*

This was Nan. Her hero. Besides, this morning she was too tired to get angry. A good thing, perhaps.

Kit loved her grandmother. She was in her sixties. but looked much younger. Her hair was short and gray, her eyes a soft blue that seemed to hold wisdom. She was warm and welcoming. People always flocked to her energy and light. There was a gentleness about her, but underneath that was a toughness. Marjorie, just like everyone else, flocked to her, and Nan never saw the real person. She never saw beyond Marjorie's facade.

Kit's eyes welled up. "Listen, I got to call the detective to see when I can open up again. I also want to check on Gabby and Trunk."

Nan's face filled the screen again. "Are they okay?"

"Yes. They were locked in the room where she died. Covered in blood and frosting."

"That's terrible. Who would leave them in there like that?"

"The murderer."

Nan looked puzzled. "Yes, I suppose so. Are the rest of the cats okay?"

"Yes. A cop was going to keep an eye on them last night. They wanted to keep them away from the crime scene. We're closed today and won't open until tomorrow or Tuesday."

"Did anyone contact Marjorie's family?"

Nan was the one who would think about these things. "I don't know. Maybe Kale."

Nan raised her eyebrows. "Kale?"

"The detective."

"On a first-name basis, I see." Nan sipped her tea.

Kit squeezed her eyes shut. "Please don't. It's been a difficult twenty-four hours, and I'm not in the mood."

"We should have a service for her."

Kit straightened up. "We? I'm not holding a service for that woman."

"Kitty. It's the respectful thing to do. She was an employee, and you are the director. It's not really an option."

Kit sank into her chair.

"Fine. I'll light a candle and give away free coffee or something."

"Can we dig a little deeper? Look in the top drawer of my desk. There's a name of a caterer we use. Call her and tell her I'll take care of it. The staff shouldn't have to cook. They have been through enough. Make sure you pay them for the days they missed. They should also be able to attend."

Kit was relieved. "Okay."

"Have Sarah call the funeral home. Tell them I'll pay for it."

"You're a good woman, Nan. If you only knew how horrible she was. Shit, I wouldn't bury her in a litter box if I had my way."

Nan shook her head. "Oh, Kitty. You may not have liked her, dear, but she was a dedicated employee for years. I owe her this much."

Kit wondered why her grandmother's compassion never rubbed off on her.

"I got to go, Nan. I'll keep you updated."

Nan put her cup in the air and blew Kit a kiss.

Kit closed the laptop.

"Damn it! A funeral? A service?"

She slammed her fist on the table, then grabbed her hand and rocked back and forth. Biting her lip and holding back a tear, she looked up at the ceiling.

"Karma. I get it."

CHAPTER 12

K it walked around the side of the building, past the sitting area, and into the parking lot, enjoying the warm sun hitting her face. She closed her eyes and, for a moment, she felt okay as the sun burned away all her frustrations. Until she opened her eyes and noticed the lack of people in the cat café. No one outside enjoying coffee, no one on their computer inside, and unfortunately, no one getting cat love.

She turned the corner to see a crowd of people gathered at the end of the parking lot behind yellow police tape. She walked around the lot, staying far away from the building she needed to enter.

She listened to the sounds of people. The stories they shared. Mostly half-truths and some completely false. A reporter walked toward her. Kit waved her hand and her head *no*. The woman turned back around to be swallowed by the crowd.

Oh, Detective Seaweed. She caught sight of him. *Kale. His name is Kale.* For the life of her, she couldn't remember his last name.

They locked eyes and he waved her over.

Scooting under the police tape, she joined him. "Yes, detective?" She shielded her eyes from the sun.

"Kitty, right?"

"No. Kit."

He tapped his pen on this temple. "Oh yeah, that's right."

"Can I get in to check on the cats?" Kit asked.

He looked behind at the door. "You can't come in this way. It's a crime scene."

Kit put her good hand on her hip. "I have cats that need care. What do you want me to do?"

"Well, a big dude and your friend came by last night to take the bloody ones to get cleaned."

"Yeah, that's Brian and Sarah. Good, but what about the other thirteen?"

"You have fifteen cats in here?" he said.

"Yes, I told you that last night. Ha, and I'm the one who was drunk." Kit pointed at the sign. "How could you forget? The name on the building says cat café."

He looked at her. "You're awfully spiky this morning. Did you miss your coffee?"

She didn't miss a beat. "You're awfully forgetful. Did you not take your memory enhancement medication this morning?"

"I guess I didn't." He looked down, smirking. "You can go around back and go through the cat area. Why is it called the PP Parlor? What the hell does that—"

Kit shrugged. "Your guess is as good as mine."

"We should finish by this afternoon," he said.

"Did your officer have any problems last night? Are the cats in the PP Parlor?"

He grimaced. "Yeah, about that. The police officer we put there last night has bad cat allergies. We removed him. The other officer who was going to get assigned to that area has this fear of cats. A childhood thing."

"Wait. What? You have a cop who is afraid of a little pussycat?" She shook her head. "I should have called the fire department."

His shoulders dropped. "That's just mean."

"You realize this is the reason the fire department gets more love than you guys." She lowered her voice. "What happened?"

"We didn't have anyone in there after 1 a.m."

Kit felt her blood drain down to her feet. The silence between them grew loud. The wind blew, and Kit pushed her hair off her face.

Finally, she spoke slowly. "What did you do with my cats?"

The detective put his hands up. "The cats are fine. We contained them."

"Please tell me you didn't put them in the café area. The Department of
Health—"

"No, we didn't."

When he didn't continue, she asked, "Did you arrest them? Are they in Kitty jail? Where are they?"

"We put them in the...gift shop."

Kit pushed him aside to see the gift shop window. There, hanging off one of the light fixtures, was a cat.

Kit's face was red, and her fists balled up. "Kitty-Kat Collectibles! The gift shop! What the f—"

He placed a hand on her shoulder, but she pushed it off.

"The one place that sells one-of-a-kind collectibles and organic catnip."

He looked at her. "Not our finest moment, but they look happy."

She poked his chest. "I am not happy. Your department is paying for this."

Kit sprinted past him.

"You can't go in there!"

The hell I can't.

She could hear footsteps behind her. In the window's reflection, she watched two uniformed officers dash toward her. She put her hand up to stop them.

"I'm not going in! I'm just looking."

Cupping her hands around her face, she peered into the window. She caught her breath.

"Oh. My. God."

CHAPTER 13

K it could not believe the mess. There were eight cats that she could see from the window. The shelves were half-empty, as everything that had been on them was now on the floor. A few of the cats walked and jumped from shelf to shelf, knocking things over as they went. Cats were sprawled on top of catnip toys and loose catnip. The catnip was everywhere, covering the cats. Bags of food were chewed through, and all the specialty treats opened. One cat was chewing on the plastic to get into a bag. Luckily, the expensive collectibles were in a case.

There was Daisy. She slid into a pile of catnip and slammed into a shelf. The shelf rocked a bit and Kit felt her knees buckle.

Behind her in the window, she could see the detective walk toward her.

"I've got to get in there. A cat will get hurt. This is insane. Last night I had cats covered in blood. Today they're covered in catnip."

"They look like they're having fun."

"If you weren't a cop, I would punch that smirk off your face."

His tone changed. "Okay, just having fun. I get it."

"I'm walking around to the PP Parlor. I'll go in that way and slip inside. I'll stay away from your crime scene." Kit looked him up and down.

He said nothing.

She walked away, her anger rising... *Balling up her fists, she walked back over to the detective and slammed his head into the shop window. She heard a thud and the cracking of glass. She watched with glee as blood trickled down the window. He looked up at her, fear frozen on his face as he slumped to the ground.*

Kit exhaled, and the image dissolved, back to her walking around the building. "The gift shop. What an idiot."

"I heard that," he called.

CHAPTER 14

The young cop stood by the tape near the office, not letting the cats near the scene. They were allowed to roam the rest of the Feline Foyer. Gabby sat in the middle of the room with her ears facing backward. She heard boots moving toward her.

"The next cop that picks me up, I am going to hiss at them!" She stood up, meowed, and put her tail in the air.

"Oh, this one is adorable!" the officer said as he reached over and patted Gabby on the head.

"She's so tiny. Can I pick her up?" he asked, looking at Kit.

Kit had watched the entire exchange as she walked out of the PP Parlor through the Feline Foyer to go to the shop.

"I wouldn't. She's not in a good mood. She had to have a bath last night after the murder."

"She looks so soft." He ignored Kit and picked Gabby up.

"I'm gonna hiss! Put me down!" Gabby fought the cuddle until he rubbed behind her ears.

"Oh, this is nice," she said as she purred.

"I thought you said she was gonna hiss?"

"She's a woman. Entitled to change her mind," Kit said, twirling her hair.

The cop continued to cuddle and pet Gabby until she had had enough—about a minute later. She jumped out of his arms.

"She meows a lot. Talkative," the cop said.

"You have no idea."

Gabby stood in front of Kit. Looking up, she meowed.

"I have a problem. I am not happy."

Kit looked down.

"Look at her meowing. She's so cute," the cop said.

"Stop that. Look at this." Gabby turned around.

"What is she meowing about?" the cop asked.

"Look. They cut my fur!"

"I think she's mad because they cut her fur during the processing."

"That's cute. Have her send a bill." He walked away.

Gabby hissed. "I just might. Don't think you'll ever get to scratch my ears again."

Kit bent down to Gabby. "I can't see it. Besides, it'll grow back."

Gabby spun around, trying to see the cut area. "This is bad. I got locked in that room, my fur cut, and there's still a murderer out there. What if he thinks I know who the killer is and comes after me?"

"Do you know who the killer is?"

"No, but you're going to find out who did it."

"I'm not a detective," Kit said.

Gabby jumped on a table near Kit. "Then why did you take those pictures?"

"You noticed me taking pictures, but not the person who killed Marjorie?"

Gabby looked around. "I had too much catnip," she whispered.

Kit grinned. "I see."

"I need my sock! Where's my sock?"

"What are you talking about?"

"My sock is missing. You need to find my sock and the murderer." Gabby sat and stared at Kit.

Kit's phone rang, but Gabby put her paw on it.

"Are you going to let me answer this?"

"Nan gave me that sock. It has a paw print on the side of it. It's not one of those stupid socks that the other cats carry around. Mine is special."

"Okay. I'll look for your sock."

"I'm going to create a search and rescue team. You don't seem up for the challenge. Don't get in my way, but if you see the sock, let me know."

Gabby jumped off the table. "Look for the murderer and my sock. Bye."

Gabby walked away; tail held high. Kit heard Gabby ask Mr. Nuggy, the Siamese cat, if he would help. He raised his head up and put it back down. She walked over to him and asked again. He lifted his head up again, yawned, and in a low, soft voice said, "Nothing is ever lost. Everything is already here."

"Why can't you answer my question?" Gabby hissed and walked away. "Trunk! Wait up; I need to talk to you."

Kit looked down at the phone. Brian.

She called him back, asking if he could come in for a few hours. According to Sarah, they were there late washing bloody cats. He said yes, he would after his Hallmark movie finished.

Kit put her hands to her face. The image of Brian sitting on a couch under a blanket watching the Hallmark Channel delighted her heart.

CHAPTER 15

In the distance, she heard Brian's motorcycle. He rounded the corner and parked on the only patch of pavement outside the PP Parlor's door. The parking lot back here was large but mostly a pebbled area.

He pulled off his helmet, brushing his bangs aside. He got off the bike and met Kit at the employee's back door.

"What's going on? The cats okay?" he asked.

"The cops left them in the gift shop. We have eight cats high on catnip and crap everywhere. Well, I don't know if we have crap, but we have stuff everywhere."

Brian chuckled, showing his dimples.

"Let's get to this. I'm going to check the ones that are not in the shop."

Brian walked to the back of the PP parlor and unlocked the door. Kit followed. He moved in quickly. To the right was a large gray industrial door that was partially open, supplies stacked floor to ceiling beyond it. A few feet past the door were twelve cubbyholes with cushions in each one, a few cats in them. Brian checked on them.

"Oh, we're going to need more cat litter soon," he said.

"What happened to the pallet of cat litter that was outside my door?"

He reached down to pet a gray cat. "They poop a lot."

"Okay, let me know what you need. After that, you'll have access to order your own. This area should be under a separate budget anyway."

"Oh, cool."

Kit heard a faint voice on a loop. "Rub my belly, rub my belly."

She avoided eye contact with the cats, so they didn't pick up on her gift just yet.

"Marjorie didn't want anyone to have control over any part of the budget," Brian said.

For a place that had walls of cat litter boxes, it smelled fresh. To the right of the Feline Foyer door and low to the floor were five cat doors, and near them were cubbies filled with blankets. To the left of the door was a small desk with a partition surrounding it. The walls were pale yellow with pictures of cats, motorcycles, and cats in tiny helmets on motorcycles.

Brian put food out, and all the cats in the cubbyholes jumped down.

Kit closed her eyes. She heard a few muffled noises. Not really voices but sounds. This was normal. Not every cat was crystal clear. Some were, but most sounded like they were underwater, muffled, or inaudible. Kit was relieved because fifteen cats who talked at once would be overwhelming, like a high school locker room all the time.

Kit opened her eyes. Brian was watching the cats.

"You were here last night. How did Gabby and Trunk do?"

He leaned his head back. "Trunk is easy to wash. He loves the attention. Gabby, well, she meowed the entire time and made a bigger mess."

Kit smiled. "Have the cops talked to you yet?"

"Nope." He slid by her to turn his computer on as he moved Peanut Butter off the keyboard.

"Come on, buddy. You can't sit here." Brian put the cat on the other chair beside him.

Peanut Butter stretched, looked up at Kit, and rubbed his cheek on Brian.

Brian brushed the computer keyboard clean with his hand. "Peanut Butter loves to stay back here. Humans are a bit much for him."

"Except for Leanne, right?"

Brian gave Kit a thumbs-up.

Brian swiveled in his chair. "I'm nervous. I was here late and heard nothing. Kinda unsettling. Besides, I wonder if I could have stopped it." He looked down.

"You really didn't hear anything?"

"Nothing. With the fans and the air conditioner running, I hear little back here. I kind of like it that way."

"What time did you leave last night?" Kit asked.

Brian squinted his eyes. "You trying to be a detective?"

"Gabby thinks that too."

Brian smiled, looking up at the clock. "We close at eight, but I don't think I left until about nine thirty. I did a quick pass around the foyer looking for Trunk. I like to put him in here at night since he has a hard time fitting through the cat doors.

I'm planning on fixing the hole over there." Brian pointed. "He needs his own. He also needs a diet."

"He was eating cake last night."

Brian grinned as he typed. "Yes, I know. I washed it off him."

"How was Gabby's bath?" Kit asked.

"Not easy. That girl cannot be held down."

"I can see that."

"Yup, seven pounds of catitude."

They both laughed.

"I wonder how they got locked in the room," Brian said. Distracted by a knock and the back door opening, he ran across the room to shut it.

There was another knock. "It's Detective Flowers. Can you open the door?"

"Hold on, let me make sure the cats are secure."

Brian cleared the cats and opened the door.

Detective Flowers walked in.

"You can't just open doors around here," Brian said as he went back to his computer.

"Oh, sorry about that. I keep forgetting about the cats," the detective said.

"Yes, you do," Kit said between gritted teeth.

The detective looked around and at his pad.

"Brian, can I talk to you for a few minutes?" It wasn't a suggestion.

"Yeah, but be careful where you walk. There are cats everywhere back here."

"I'll do my best."

"Best what? Cat stepping, cat avoiding, or cat corralling. So far, you're two out of three," Kit said.

The detective looked up. "Ouch. Can I have a few minutes to talk to Brian?"

"Sure. I have a mess to clean due to inappropriate cat corralling." Kit turned to walk out.

"Kit? Do you have security cameras?"

"I don't know." She turned back to look at Brian.

"No. Marjorie didn't think we needed them. Ironic, huh?" Brian swiveled his chair toward Kit.

"Isn't it ironic?" Kit sang as she left the room.

CHAPTER 16

K it found herself in the middle of the demolished gift shop. Gabby crouched outside the glass door, scratching at the bottom of it as fast as she could.

"Can I come in? Can I? Can I?"

"Not now," Kit said in a firm tone.

"I smell the catnip." Gabby sniffed the air as she pawed harder at the door.

"No!"

"You're mean!"

"I'm not mean. I have a mess to clean, and I don't want you under my feet." She stepped over Daisy, who was rolling around in catnip. The white cat looked stoned.

"Daisy? You in there?" Gabby's voice was muffled by the door.

Daisy raised her head, looked in the wrong direction, and put it back down again. Catnip fell from her whiskers. "Meeeooow."

"Is my cat sock in there?" Gabby stalked back and forth in front of the glass windows and door. "Do you see it?"

Daisy rolled and stretched in the catnip, then stuck her face in the pile. Kit heard her inhale.

"Aww, come on, Daisy," Gabby said.

She hissed and began scratching at the door again. "Let me in!"

"No," Kit said.

"You're a mean human."

Kit shrugged her shoulders. "I know. You said that already."

"If I was a monkey, I'd throw poop at you."

Kit laughed.

She narrowed her eyes. "I'm serious."

Kit chuckled. "Gabby, I'll look for your sock. Let me do my work."

Gabby hissed and walked away. "I'm done with you. You're dead to me. Like the last mouse I killed."

Kit giggled, knowing she was in earshot of Gabby. "Ah, peace. Finally!"

Gabby twitched her tail.

Kit moved around the shop, stepping over all the things that had fallen on the floor. Occasionally, she would brush a flying piece of cat fur away from her face.

"I'll never find a cat sock in here," she said to herself.

She moved a cat toy off the floor and realized there was a cat holding on to the other end.

Big pleading eyes looked up at her.

"You must be Vee. Come on, girl." Kit reached down to grab the feather from her.

"It's my feather. Let go," Vee said.

Kit heard her as clear as day.

"Yes, Vee. It's your feather, but I need it for a bit."

"It's mine."

Vee put the feather in her mouth and looked at Kit with her big yellow eyes again.

Kit melted. *So adorable.*

"Vee, you are a good girl. Fine, keep the feather."

Kit turned around as another cat slid across the floor, knocking over the remaining box of cat cookies.

Kit sat down in the middle of the room. She saw the cops outside, the yellow tape, and a few vans. Channel 7 and Channel 13 were there.

The crowd had doubled from just an hour ago.

She listened to the hum of the people and the TV announcer.

"We are live at Caddy Cat Café..."

Kit's mind drifted to the image of the crime scene. She remembered how Gabby and Trunk looked with all the blood, frosting, and bits of catnip stuck to them. She even recalled how the frosting made Trunk more pink than red, especially on his side. He must have fallen into the cake.

A tap on the door startled her back to reality. Detective Flowers stood in the door. He mouthed, "Can I come in?"

She put up one finger as she carefully got up, carefully moving around the cats who were slipping and sliding in catnip.

When he stepped inside, a squeak came from below his feet. "Did I step on a cat?"

"No, just a toy."

He looked around. "Sorry about this."

"Yeah. Are you finished with Brian? I can't get anything done until we can move the cats back to that room."

"Yes, but I'll need to talk with you this afternoon," he said.

"I'll be here all day long." Her phone began ringing.

"Yes?"

"Kitty, this is Brenda Converse calling to set up an appointment."

Kit rubbed her eyes. "I don't have time for this right now. Can we postpone it? Maybe next month?"

"No. The judge ordered mandatory sessions to begin right away. I have given you time to return to Massachusetts and get settled."

"There was just a murder in my coffee shop."

"I'm sorry to hear about that. Even better reason to come see me," Brenda said.

"I'll call you later."

"Don't hang up—"

Kit put the phone back in her pocket. "Sorry about that."

"It seems important."

"Everything seems important right now, but not everything is."

"Okay, give us another hour. We want to do another quick sweep around the room. Then you can clean it up."

Kit dropped her shoulders. "Clean it up? The bloody room?"

"Um, if you need it, I can give you the name of a company that cleans up. It will look as good as new."

She exhaled. "Yes. Please. I can't make my employees clean up another bloody mess. The cats were enough."

"I'll text you the number," he said, walking out of the room.

Kit saw Brian heading toward the door. He had a cat carrier tucked under each arm and two in each hand. The detective met him in the middle of the Feline Foyer. They nodded at each other, and he continued on.

Kit navigated the obstacle course of cats and toys to open the door wide for Brian, blocking any cats from going in or out.

Brian dropped the cat carriers. "Holy cat shit, this is a mess!"

"It's crowded in here too." Kit felt claustrophobic, even though she was surrounded by windows and glass doors.

A light flashed. "Great. No makeup, and now I'm on the evening news."

Brian looked at her with a flat expression. "I won't tell you about the catnip hanging off your hair."

"Great," she said, turning away from the window.

Brian smiled and waved at the reporters.

"Nice to be photogenic. Work it, dude."

"I am. Picture this." He spread his hands in the air. "Cats Gone Wild. We can have a sale and make this benefit us."

Kit beamed. "Great idea. I'll take a few pictures before we clean up. We can restock and be ready in a few weeks."

"Despite all this BS, having you here has been refreshing. Marjorie wasn't open to much." Brian began picking up boxes of cat treats and placing them back on the rack.

Kit took pictures, zooming her phone in on the cats.

"I'm sorry she died the way she did, but I'm not sad she's gone," Kit said.

"Yeah, that seems to be the consensus. Have you met Craig?"

"No, who is he?"

Brian held up a half-empty bag of cat treats. "He's our delivery guy, and he's been making these cat cookies and selling them. He's hoping to start a company. I heard they're good. The cats love them. I think he's supposed to drop some off today. Did anyone tell him not to deliver? We should have him make more for the sale."

"Good question. Ask Sarah. The detective said he'll leave today. We'll be closed tomorrow. I need to call that cleaning service for the break room. Should be done by Tuesday."

"Good. I could use an extra day to get organized." He put a cat in a carrier.

"Listen, I want to help you in here, but I can't do much with my hand."

"No sweat, I'll get on my guys to help."

A calico cat flew by his feet. "That's Vee. She found a feather, huh?"

"And she won't let it go," Kit said.

"She owns it now."

Kit looked at Vee. Really cute but hard to hear with a feather in her mouth.

CHAPTER 17

E yes wide, mouth open with a look of terror on his face, Craig's blond hair was a mess and his clothes wrinkled from sitting for too long.

A moment before, Brian had tapped on the window of Kitty Cat Collectibles to tell Kit that Craig had arrived.

He stood behind the police tape, his van parked off to the side. Kit waved at Craig and pointed for him to go around to the back of the building.

Craig pulled up fast behind Brian's bike. *Why do these young people drive so fast? Another issue for another time.*

He jumped out of the van. Kit shook his hand and introduced herself.

His eyes darted around. "What's going on?" he asked.

"You didn't hear?" Kit asked. "Someone killed Marjorie last night."

Craig leaned hard against his van. "She was alive when I left. Oh my god! They're going to think I did it!"

She put her hand on his shoulders. "Take a deep breath, Craig. The police have to talk to you if you were there last night. What time did you leave?"

He shifted his weight. "Are you a detective now?"

"Why is everyone asking me that? I'm like a cat—curious."

"Around eight twenty. I gave her a sample of my new cat cookies. She seemed to like them. She told me she was going to order the new flavor and more of the old flavors I'd created." He paused. "How did Marjorie die?"

Kit leaned on the van next to him. "Stabbed."

He looked directly into her eyes. "I swear she was alive when I left." His voice trembled.

"Just tell the detective the truth, and you'll be fine." Kit looked back at the van. "Don't worry about the order today. You can bring them by Tuesday. We'll get more cookies from you. Talk to Sarah about that in a few days."

"Okay," he said.

"One more thing."

Craig's eyes widened.

"Did you put the cat litter in front of my door last week?"

"Yeah. Marjorie told me to, said the other room was full," he said.

"That door was to my apartment." She held her hand up. "I slammed into the boxes in the morning. Broke my hand."

He pushed off the van and covered his face with his palm. "I'm—I didn't know. I'm so sorry."

Kit twirled her hair. "Not your fault. Marjorie knew. From now on, all boxes go to the PP Parlor supply room except for the cat cookies. You can display them yourself. But not today. The gift shop is a mess."

"When are you going to need those cat cookies? It takes time to make them."

"No rush. We're planning a sale in a month to recoup some losses from damage to the shop."

"Okay. It was nice meeting you. Wish it wasn't at a bad time. Again, sorry about your hand."

"Thanks, Craig. You better go talk to the detective. Otherwise, he'll track you down."

"I will," he said, looking down at his feet.

CHAPTER 18

K it sat straight up from a dead sleep.

"What was that?" she whispered to herself. She tried to listen beyond the pounding of her heart. Another bang, this time metal on metal.

That was not a cat.

Her hands shook as she reached for the phone and dialed 911.

"I think someone broke into my shop," Kit said in a low voice. She listened to the operator while trying to listen to sounds outside her apartment.

"Yes, that is correct, Caddy Cat Café. No, it sounded like it was in the kitchen. The cats don't have access in there. Yes, I live in the back, in the apartment."

Kit jumped. Another bang, this time louder.

"They're still here," she whispered.

"I said they're still here. Yes, I hear the sirens."

Kit got out of bed, scurried to the bathroom, and locked the door. She realized at that moment that she would be trapped if the intruder came into her apartment. She unlocked the door and walked back into her bedroom, listening.

She gripped the phone tight. "I don't hear the sirens anymore. Yes, that makes sense. I don't want them scared away, either."

"They got him. Oh, that's great." Kit plopped on her bed. "I'll see if I know him, sure. I'll meet them at the door of my apartment."

Kit hung up the phone and wiped her face.

"I've never had so much anxiety working in a cat café. Jeez!" she said out loud as she walked into her dining room. The cop pulled into her driveway at the far end of her apartment.

She noticed a slender figure in the back of the cruiser but couldn't make out the person. An overweight officer stepped out from behind the wheel, adjusted his pants, and walked over to her sliding glass door.

She greeted him.

"Are you Kitty Beck?" he asked.

"Yes. You have him?"

"Yup, but it's not a him. I'll bring her out of the car. You up for it?"

"Her?"

"Yes, ma'am. The noise you heard was her falling over the pans in the kitchen. She said she works here. Something about leaving keys in her locker?"

"That makes no sense. Um, who is she?"

"Janice Jordan?"

"Janice. Yes, she works here. She's our cook."

"Okay, well, she had a key, so she got in, but she also went through the side door and into the crime scene. I'm going to call the detective."

"I don't know what the detective will do."

"Do you want to press charges?"

"No, officer. She's a good kid, just not that bright. I'll keep her here until I hear from the detective." Kit half smiled.

"Alright." He walked over and let Janice out of the back of the cruiser. She stepped out, wiping a tear from her eye as she walked up to the apartment. Kit waved at the officer as he left the scene.

Kit felt like a mother with a child coming home late. Her good hand was on her hip.

"What were you thinking? You scared me. You could have called first, Janice."

"Kit, I'm so sorry." She walked in and sat on the couch. "I forgot my key, and I knew they wouldn't let me in because of the crime scene."

"Janice, what key?"

"My house key." She slumped back.

Kit pressed her hand to her forehead. "Damn. A murderer is loose, and you think it's a good idea to break in?" She paused. "If you lost your house key, how did you get into this building?"

"I'm sorry—"

"I should fire you right now!"

Kit's face was flushed. She paced in the kitchen for a moment. "Okay, stop with the bullshit about the key. I saw you spinning it on your finger the other day. It was the same one you used to get in here. They're all on one key ring."

Janice widened her eyes. "Wow, you caught that?"

"Why are you here, Janice?"

Janice turned her gaze away and took a breath. "I'm sorry. Please don't fire me. I love it here. It's just—"

"Damn it, Janice!"

"I'm in trouble. I lied to the cops."

"What kinda lie?" Kit eyed the door, wondering if she should be near it.

"Janice, did you kill Marjorie?"

Janice looked back at Kit. "No."

Kit could sense she was not telling the truth about something. "Since you are going to be here a bit, do you want something to drink?"

"Yeah, you got soda?"

"Yup." Kit got her a soda and sat next to her on the couch.

"Alright, spill," Kit said.

"I know who killed Marjorie."

Kit's mouth opened, but no words came out.

Janice adjusted her glasses. "I was here the other night, and I heard Marjorie and Craig arguing about something. Plus, she was drunk. So, it was loud. He left, and when he did, he slammed the side door."

She played with her nails. "I was ready to leave. I walked past the room and saw Marjorie slumped over. I panicked. He's my good friend, Kit. I don't want to get him in trouble." She looked at Kit.

"Go on."

"Well, I saw a bag of catnip and a bag of cookies on the table. He makes specialty treats. We call them cookies. I took them and hid them in my locker. I thought if the cops found them, they would know it was him." She sniffed. "I was going to take them home tonight, but there were too many cops around, so I couldn't. But when I got home, I realized they might search my locker, find them, and think I did it. So I came back. I forgot I left the pans on the table to dry. That was the bang."

Janice took a sip of soda.

"The break room door was closed," Kit said.

"Yeah, I did that. It freaked me out to see her staring at me. I shut the door." Janice rubbed her shoulders.

"Why would he kill her?"

"I'm not saying he did, but Marjorie has always been nasty. Even when he gave her the cookies, she was nasty to him. Like she was doing him a favor. Maybe he was tired of it. I didn't hear what they were arguing about. Marjorie was slurring her words. I've learned to tune her out."

"You have to tell the cops, Janice."

Janice shook her head fast. "No. No. My prints are on the bag. I just grabbed them."

"Was there blood on the bags?"

"I don't know."

"Janice, where are the bags now?"

"In my locker still. As soon as that first pan hit the floor, I panicked. I froze."

Kit looked at her phone, which was now on the table. There was a message from Detective Flowers. He was on his way. *Be there in ten.*

"Well, the detective is on his way."

"You called him!" Janice stood up.

"No. Sit back down. The other officer called him because you entered a crime scene."

She sat back down and ran her fingers through her hair. Her hands trembled.

"Janice, just tell the truth, that's all."

Janice sobbed.

CHAPTER 19

A knock on the door. As Kit looked out, she could see a disheveled man with hair in all directions at the apartment window. Kit opened the door.

"Where is she?" Detective Flowers asked, walking in.

Kit put her bandaged hand up. He stopped.

"She is freaking out. Please go gentle."

"Kit, it's three in the morning. I'm a little irritated, but I'll go *gentle*." He used air quotes.

"Ms. Jordan. What the hell were you doing breaking into your place of employment at 2:30 in the morning?"

"Seriously, this is gentle?"

He ignored Kit. "I could have you arrested for destroying a crime scene."

"Detective!"

The detective turned around and stood there for a minute. He turned back to Janice, his tone softer.

"Why did you come back here tonight?"

Janice looked at Kit, who nodded. "I was getting something out of my locker. A bag of catnip and cat cookies that Craig left in the break room."

He sat on the coffee table directly in front of Janice. "So let me get this straight. You had evidence in your locker that you did not tell us about?"

Janice nodded.

"You broke in tonight to take that evidence out? Where are the bags now?"

"In my locker," she whispered.

Detective Flowers pulled out his phone and made a call.

"I'm going to have one of my team members pick them up. Is your locker locked?"

"Yes."

"Give me the key."

Janice took the key off the ring.

"Why were there cookies back there?"

"Craig brought a bag of catnip for the cats and cookies for Marjorie to test. She liked to take a bite out of them," Janice said.

The detective frowned.

"They're all-natural ingredients. She figured if she could eat them, it's safe for the cats."

"How did you know the cat cookies were in the break room? The door was closed."

"I heard Craig and Marjorie arguing. She sounded drunk, so I ignored them. When I went to leave, I walked past the break room, saw her slumped over, and panicked. I grabbed the catnip and cookies and shut the door."

"You didn't think to call 911."

"No, sir."

"You left the cats in the room?"

"I didn't see the cats," Janice said.

"Alright." The detective slapped his legs as he got up. "I need you to come with me down to the station. I need to print you and get a formal statement. We also need to discuss your alibi after the murder."

Janice chugged the soda and stood up.

Kit called the detective away from Janice, out of earshot.

"Did you talk to Craig?"

"Not yet."

"He was at the café today. I told him to wait for you, that you might have questions."

"I'll track him down today. It's getting late, or early," the detective said.

He returned to Janice.

"Are you arresting me?" she asked.

"No, not yet. But you might be in trouble, young lady."

"Craig is going to hate me. He's my best friend," she said.

"You need to worry about yourself right now. Let's go."

"Can I go with her?" Kit asked.

"You can't come in when I talk to her, but you can wait. It might take a while."

"That's okay. She looks terrified." Kit glanced at Janice.

"Alright, meet us there."

It had to be late, or early as the detective put it, because the sun had risen a few minutes ago. Kit looked down at her empty paper cup.

She heard the door open and walked toward the detective.

"Well?" she said.

"I don't know. What she did was suspicious, and I need to check her alibi. She'll be here a while."

"Were there any prints on the knife?" Kit asked.

"No. Just Marjorie's. Wait. Why are you asking these questions?"

Kit considered her answer for a moment.

"I saw Craig the day I first arrived. He was putting these cookies on a display shelf in the Kitty Cat Collectibles. You know, the place your officers destroyed."

He rolled his eyes. "Can't live that down."

"Anyway, he had gloves on."

The detective looked off to the side.

"This party they had on Friday. What time was Marjorie there at? Was Craig there?"

"I don't remember seeing them, but I'd just started, and I'm still putting faces with names. Ask Sarah; she'll know," Kit said.

"Are you heading home? I'll get Janice home later."

"Is she arrested?"

"No. Don't have any proof that she killed her. I can charge her with tampering with evidence, but I haven't done so yet. I'm waiting for the bags to be processed. And I need to talk to Craig."

He paused.

"Go home, Kit. It's late. or early, whatever you prefer."

He walked away.

CHAPTER 20

"Hi, Nan." Kit twirled her hair, getting it stuck between her fingers.

"Hi, dear. How are you doing?"

"It's been a rough few days."

"How are the cats?"

"The cats are great. They had a party in the collectibles shop."

"Oh, that's lovely."

Kit shook her head. Her grandmother wasn't paying attention.

Kit drifted off in thought. Her grandmother was going on about handsome blokes.

Kit scrunched her nose when her grandmother mentioned she was returning. "What?"

"Yes, I'm thinking of returning to the states for a few days."

"Why?"

"You shouldn't have to deal with this situation alone," Nan said.

Kit's mind spun. *Does she think I can't handle it? Will it make me look weak if my grandmother returns and takes over?*

"Kit?"

"Nan, you don't have to return. I got it. Everyone is supportive, and there's nothing you can do. Unless you want to take over Marjorie's service."

"Oh, poor Marjorie. Poor Marjorie."

Kit clenched her jaw. "No, Nan. Not poor Marjorie. Poor us who had to deal with her! Why are you taking her side? She locked me in my frigging apartment. I had a hand broken by her. She intimidated her staff and was mean to them. Did you know that everyone the detective talked to said they hated her? Did you know that?"

Nan kept quiet.

Finally, she said, "Okay. Well, I guess we see people differently, don't we?"

"Only you saw her as kind; no one else. She was a rotten bi—"

"Okay. I understand. We will talk about that later."

Just like her grandmother to change the subject.

"Alright, dear, I need to get back to the deck. I've got some skeet shooting to do. If you need me to come back, let me know soon."

"I'm good." Kit hung up and screamed into her sleeve.

CHAPTER 21

"I need you to listen to me," Gabby said.

The Feline Foyer looked like the remains of a party, cats sprawled out from too much playing and catnip.

Daisy walked over to Gabby. She stopped, yawned, and sat down.

Trunk licked a wall, not paying attention.

"What are you doing?" Gabby padded over to Trunk and paw-popped him on the head. "Stop that. You don't know what's been there."

Trunk ignored her and kept on licking.

"Mr. Nuggy, are you joining us?" Gabby asked.

Mr. Nuggy opened his blue eyes and shut them again. "Yes, Miss Gabby. Give me a moment," he said in a slow tone.

"Vee? Where are you? Why isn't anyone listening to me?" Gabby jumped from seat to table to finally settle on the cushion in the room's corner.

"Maybe it's because you're yelling at us. Again," Daisy said.

"I'm yelling because no one is listening. Again." Gabby eyed Daisy.

"What is this about?" Trunk said as he plopped down in front of Gabby.

"Alright." Gabby paced back and forth. "As you know, we had a human murder."

"Yeah, no loss to us," Vee said as she padded over and scratched her back. Her fur rained. Trunk caught it and tried to lick it. He ran a paw over his mouth.

"Pfft."

Gabby made a fake cough. "Are you done?" she said to Trunk.

"Talk to her. She's the one who shed all over me!"

Vee whirled.

"Do you know who killed her, Gabby? You were in the room. It would devastate me to get that much blood on my fur," Daisy said.

"No, I only saw boots. I was too busy enjoying the catnip."

Trunk leaned on his back paws. "You were playing with the knife. You had frosting and catnip all over your face."

"Trunk, you didn't look better. Can we pay attention, please!" Gabby hissed.

"I am so upset. I was carrying my sock. I got distracted by the catnip. When I went to look for it today, it was gone! It was a white sock with a black paw print on it. It was catnip-scented," Gabby said, lowering her chin.

Mr. Nuggy opened his eyes slowly. "Catnip, ahh. The addiction continues. You will never be mindful if you are chasing the nip."

Daisy lifted her head. "Gabby, you can get another one in the gift shop. Well, once they let us back in."

"Yeah, you should know. You made the mess in there," Gabby said.

Daisy stood up. "It wasn't just me! I had to taste the cookies, and they left catnip out. What's a girl to do?"

Trunk eyed Daisy's collar, thin green rhinestones with a silver charm moving ever so slightly.

He snuck over, tipped his head, and hit the charm.

"Trunk, stop playing with my necklace!"

"It's not a necklace. It's a collar," Gabby said.

Daisy puffed out her chest. "I am not a dog. It's a necklace."

Trunk plopped back down.

Gabby went back to her discussion, stomping her paw. "Will you listen to me? This is a special sock. Nan gave it to me. It's my favorite, and I want it back." She sat back down on the cushion.

Trunk rolling over. "Do you think that cop took it?"

Gabby lowered her voice. "I don't know. I didn't see it after I saw the boot."

"You think the boot took it?" Vee asked as she reached down to put her paw on Daisy's head.

Daisy looked up. "Stop it. You'll mess up my fur."

"Pay attention," Gabby said.

"Gabby, we are cats. Our attention is as fleeting as feathers on the wind," Mr. Nuggy said, staring off into the distance.

Vee stood up. "Did someone mention a feather? Where?" She spun around to look.

"No feather, Vee, just a missing sock," Daisy said.

"I don't want to get my tail in a bunch over this. I just need my sock! Who will help me look?" She narrowed her eyes at everyone.

Vee pointed to a white cat across from them, staring at a wall. "Why don't you ask Fluffy, whatever his name is, to help you find your sock?"

"See, Daisy. She doesn't know his name either." Gabby stuck her tongue out at Daisy.

Daisy shook her head. "His name is Fluffy Bottom. I've told you this a hundred times."

"Well, Fluffy Butt is useless. He can't find a pickle in a pickle jar," Gabby said.

"I don't know why I bother," Daisy said.

Trunk meowed as he rolled over to lick the chair leg. "I'll look tomorrow. It's late. I need my catnap."

"Really? You're going to lick the chair legs now?" Gabby said.

Vee looked down from the table at Trunk. "I agree with Mr. Licker. I'm tired. I chased a lot of feathers."

"Me too," Daisy chimed in. "Well, not feathers, but I did way too much catnip."

"Yes, I am going to head back to my cushion to meditate on this. I'll look in the morning," Mr. Nuggy said.

"Fine! I'll go look by myself. You're all useless. We should replace every one of you with dogs. At least they aim to please."

"All of this for a sock?" Daisy asked.

"Daisy, what would you do for a new collar? I know what I would do for a feather," Vee said.

Daisy shrugged her shoulders. "I suppose."

Trunk stopped licking the chair leg. "I'm telling you, it's not the sock. It's the catnip. We might need an intervention," he said.

"Said the boy who licks everything," Daisy said.

"Let's be kind to Miss Gabby. This is not about a sock. She needs to find her inner purr." Mr. Nuggy watched Gabby search under the couch.

CHAPTER 22

M onday was a better day. Kit worked with Sarah all day to finish organizing Kitty Cat Collectibles. The cleaning company got the break room cleaned up. You would never know there was a murder in there. At almost dinner time, since they were not yet open, Kit sent everyone home.

Trunk lay around most of the day. Kit could hear him saying, "Sit. Sit. Sit." It never changed. Three words. She wondered if he said anything else.

Gabby padded around the Feline Foyer. She was on a mission to find her sock. She babbled to herself, "Where is my sock? I need my sock."

"Gabby, where are you going so fast?" Kit reached down to grab her. The cat slid between her hands. Kit took a step forward and caught her.

"Put me down! I need my sock."

Kit rubbed her chin. "Oh, that's nice," Gabby said, leaning into Kit.

Carrying Gabby, Kit tugged on the front door to make sure it was locked, being careful not to hurt her hand.

Shifting her weight, Kit whispered in Gabby's ear.

"What's going on, little girl?"

Gabby purred and ignored Kit as she settled into the human arms. "I know it's late, but let's go to the office for a few. I need to get some work done.

"Good, I can look for my sock in the office."

"Yes, you can look for your sock."

Kit dropped Gabby on an empty section of the couch. Kit went to the desk and focused on the computer.

Gabby started pawing at the couch, sticking her nose in everything. She even jumped up on shelves, pushing paper all over the place.

Kit looked up from the computer, grinning. "Gabby, I don't think it's up on the shelf."

"I don't care what you think! I need my sock." She jumped into a box.

Kit stopped typing. "You're being mean, Gabby."

"I live with lazy cats. Not one of them is searching for my sock." She poked her head out of the box. "And you're sitting on your butt, not helping either."

Kit chuckled. "Okay, little one. I'll find you a sock."

"No. Not a sock, *my* sock."

Okay. Kit got up and looked around the sofa.

"I already looked over there," Gabby said.

"The only cat I can have a full conversation with is demanding."

Getting on the floor, she bent down to look under the bookshelf. Almost banging into Gabby's butt, she moved to the other side.

"You're in my way!"

"Gabby, you're being rude. Either you want my help or not," Kit said.

"You're too big. I can't see beyond your butt."

"My butt is not big."

Gabby looked around the table. "Yeah, if you say so."

"It's not big! Oh my god, I'm arguing with a cat."

"I think you need anger management." Gabby turned away to inspect the other side of the room.

"Gabby, you will get more people to help you if you give kindness and not hisses."

"Yeah, like you did with Marjorie?"

"Fine, go find your sock on your own." Kit climbed up from the floor and returned to the desk. "Besides, that is different."

"No, it's not different. Us cats are better. We tell it like it is, and we are direct. If you would have just smelled her butt, you would have known the person she truly was."

Kit leaned on the desk. "Humans don't smell butts, Gabby."

"I know. I can't get any of you to smell mine, and I stick my butt in everyone's face."

"Well, stop doing that. No more butts in faces."

"Whatever. It's not here. I'm going to leave you to do whatever you do," Gabby said.

"Good luck with your search."

Gabby padded out of the office. If a cat could flip you off, she would have at that moment.

Kit sat there surrounded by piles of paperwork, binders, and whatever else Marjorie was working on. It was hard to tell with the mess. She looked up at the clock. Eleven thirty.

Standing up, she pushed all the paperwork onto the floor. Everything.

She sat on the floor and started separating everything into piles. Out of nowhere, the pile moved as Gabby slid into the middle of it.

"Gabby!"

Gabby looked up with a piece of paper on her head.

"Seriously?"

"What?" Gabby asked as she pushed more paper around.

"You just messed up my piles." Kit laughed. She picked up the stack of discarded paper and plopped Gabby in the middle of it. "Here, you can go wild in this pile."

"Sweet," Gabby said, rolling around, tucking her paws under the papers.

Out of the corner of her eye, Gabby saw Trunk enter the room. He plopped on the paper, stretching out.

"Hey, get off me!" she hissed.

"Sit. Sit. Sit."

"So many words, Trunk," Kit said.

"He talks to me," Gabby said.

"Does he know who committed the murder?"

"Nope," Gabby said as she rubbed her head on the paper.

Kit got up, grabbed a few receipts, and put them into the computer. She noticed the Post-it with "LITTER" she saw in the window the other day.

"She knew he was running out of cat litter. She was playing a game." Kit moved the note. The next one struck her hard.

"Leave me out of this" was written in a bold script.

She stared in disbelief. She jumped up, grabbed a note Marjorie had written, and compared it.

This is not Marjorie's handwriting.

Kit went to the filing cabinet, pulled thirty staff file folders, and dropped them on the floor with a clunk. She dove into each of them. By the eleventh, her eyes closed as she sank against the computer table.

"Damn it." Kit looked at Gabby and Trunk, who were now sleeping. The clock said two-fifteen. Wide awake, she made coffee, then dug into the pile of receipts that were in a bin.

Something felt off. The receipt dated the day Marjorie died was for the cat cookies. She shuddered, realizing this was the last receipt she wrote.

She matched it with other receipts for Craig's cat cookies, figuring out Marjorie's system. Marjorie put a letter D in a circle for a receipt that was a partial deposit on an item. This one had no D.

Going through the rest of the invoices, there was no D anywhere on Craig's paperwork. Kit stopped and took a sip of coffee. She looked in the register. No other invoices or payments to him.

"Huh."

In the morning, she would revisit this. She picked up her coffee cup, flicked the lights out, and left the office door ajar so she wouldn't wake the sleeping cats. She tiptoed out the door and down the hall to her apartment.

CHAPTER 23

Tipping her head to the left as she twirled her hair, Kit looked at the table. She'd made a memorial table for Marjorie. Nan's suggestion. The display was right outside her office on the sideboard. The same table she'd grabbed her wine from a few days before.

She covered the table with a white cloth, added a white candle burning in a lantern, a picture of Marjorie, and next to that, a bouquet of roses. On the other end was some food and a punch bowl. Keeping the cats away from the display would be another story.

Leanne walked by.

"So s-sad," she said with a genuine expression on her face. It surprised Kit, considering the way Marjorie had treated her.

"Maybe you can help, Leanne. Something is missing, but I can't figure out what it is."

Leanne stood there for what felt like forever.

"It l-looks g-good. How about a b—b-book for the f-family to s-sign."

"That's it!" Kit said, raising her hands.

"Leanne, can I ask you something?"

Leanne looked up without saying a word.

"You're very kind to Marjorie's memory, even though she was mean to you. How come?"

"Ahh, she learned her lesson now," she said in a clear voice, which took Kit aback.

"What do you mean?" Kit was almost afraid to ask.

"She's in h-heaven. She's f-for-given."

Kit smiled at the simplicity of that statement and the kindness of the girl's heart. *If only I could be half as kind.*

Leanne leaned over and gave Kit one of her hugs that lasted forever. Pulling away was fruitless.

"I like purple. Are you keeping it for a while?" she asked as Leanne finally let go.

Leanne grabbed a tiny strand of hair and looked at it. "I d-don't know. My -mom said it-it brings out m-my eyes."

Your eyes are brown, but I'll go with it. "Yes, I would agree."

Kit moved to the left, behind a high table, to prevent another hug. A cat walked up and headbutted her leg.

"What color is next?"

"You'll have to-to wait and see," Leanne said, walking away.

"Don't forget to sign the book."

"Okay," Leanne said.

Kit pursed her lips as she grabbed the menu on the table. Watching the clock, she could feel her nerves getting the best of her.

"Hey. Good morning, Kit," Sarah said. She sat at the table, and Kit could smell her shampoo.

"Good morning. I've been waiting for you."

Sarah's eyes went wide. "Am I late? Did I miss something?"

"No, nothing like that. Once you get settled, meet me in my office." Kit looked over her shoulder. "I found something. About the murder."

"Okay, give me five minutes. I'll meet you there. You want a coffee?"

"Sure, that sounds great. Light with—"

"I know what you like," Sarah said.

Kit smiled as Daisy meandered by. She padded by so slowly and deliberately.

"Meow," she said as if she were greeting the staff.

"Hey, what's the matter?" Kit asked Daisy as two women stopped in front of them.

Without missing a beat, Kit said, "Good morning, ladies. Are you enjoying your time here?"

"Yes. Were you talking to the cat?" the older woman asked.

"Yes, she seems cranky, and I'm not getting much out of her."

Daisy looked up.

The women looked at each other, then petted Daisy. "She's pretty."

"Yes, she is. Perhaps you'll have your coffee on that green bench and call her over. She could use some attention."

"Oh, lovely. Come on, kitty," the older woman said. Daisy followed, but she still moved slowly.

Sarah walked around the corner.

"Did you get the pen and signing book for Marjorie's memorial?" Kit asked.

"Oh my god, I thought you wanted a full-length cutout of Marjorie. It's in my car. I didn't even think of the guest book."

Kit opened her mouth. "Are you serious?"

Sarah had a flat expression but then burst out laughing. "You should see your face. I'm messing with you. But we could get a T-rex cutout. That would be funny."

Kit scowled. "The other cutout would have given me nightmares."

Sarah put the book and pen on the table. "We all would have had nightmares. This table looks great, Kit."

"Thanks. No one's come over here except for Leanne. "

"Did she hug you?"

"Yes, but only a side hug, not enough to squish my liver."

"Good, she's been known to hold on for dear life," Sarah said.

Sarah put her coffee down and sat on the couch. She was wearing her hunter-green smock over a cute white shirt and blue pants. Her small frame allowed her to wear just about anything, including a paper bag.

Kit began talking fast. "I was going through some paperwork last night. Marjorie made money, but her process was shit. I had to dump everything on the floor and go through all the files. I found a few weird things. First, this note." Kit handed it to Sarah.

"I don't understand. What is this?"

"Did you read it?"

"'Leave me out of this.' What does this mean?" Sarah asked.

"It's Janice's handwriting, and considering she broke into the kitchen to take back the catnip..."

Sarah whispered, "Do you think Janice killed her?"

"I don't think so, but she knows more than she's telling."

"Does the detective know about this?"

"No." Kit scooted closer Sarah. "There's more. Look at this receipt."

"Yeah, that's a receipt for a down payment for the cat cookies that Craig makes."

"Yes, now look at these two. Also supposed to be down payments from his previous deliveries, right?"

"He told me Marjorie gave him down payments."

"Here's the thing." Kit held the receipts up. "There's no symbol on this one from the night of the murder, and there's no D on these two. I can't find any other payable receipts that show she paid him anything."

Sarah yanked the receipts out of Kit's hand. "You're right! Marjorie always put a D on everyone's receipt if it was a down payment. So why—?"

"I think she promised him more money for the other shipments but never paid."

"They were arguing the other day. I saw them right before the party we had for you. Good reason as any to want her dead."

"The poor kid's trying to start a business." Kit shook her head. "Marjorie was rotten."

Sarah groaned. "This is so strange. We're walking around here, and a murderer could work with us."

"I know. It unnerves me too. I'm going to talk to Janice today. She knows more than she told me."

CHAPTER 24

G abby had walked around the Feline Foyer five times, looking under tables, chairs, behind furniture, in the PP Parlor, plus she looked as best she could through the window into the café. She even tried to get into the kitchen, which irritated Janice. Finally, she stomped into the office.

Kit was on the phone, ignoring her as she looked around. The quest to find her sock continued. Walking out, she meowed loudly.

Padding over to Daisy, she asked, "Have you looked for my sock?"

Daisy looked up from a nap. "Um, I looked over there."

"Looked where? Over by that couch, the one Leanne sits on?"

"I guess." Daisy dropped her head back down, only to pick it up quickly when Gabby got in her face.

"You're not helping! I thought you were going to help me?"

"I'm exhausted. I played with a kid today. He made me chase a feather around and around and around..."

"Thanks a lot, Daisy," Gabby said, padding away.

She made two more laps, this time slower, until she ran into Trunk getting ready to lick a wall.

"Trunk, have you looked for my sock?"

"What sock?"

"My sock that's been missing, the sock I told you about. You were going to help me look for it."

"Oh, that sock," Trunk said, sniffing a wall.

"You can spot a smell on a wall to sniff and lick like a weirdo, but you can't smell the catnip in my sock." Gabby looked at him sideways. She poked a paw into his side.

"Gabby, there is catnip everywhere. With your catnip addiction, I'm surprised you can't smell it. Did you ask Vee or Mr. Nuggy if they found your sock?"

Gabby removed her paw from his side. "No. Vee's been hanging out with anyone who will give her attention and Mr. Nuggy's been watching a bird."

Trunk stopped sniffing as his eyes got wider. "A bird? Where?"

"In the tree outside the wind—"

Trunk bolted up and sprinted to the window.

"Geez, what's up with birds? Never seen him run that fast, not even for dinner."

Gabby walked over to the long cushion near the cat café, laid down, and tucked her paws under her body. She watched the other cats playing and having fun, all except for her. Her friends, well, supposed friends, were too busy to help her. The one human who could understand her was busy in the office. She closed her eyes and soon fell asleep.

A voice at her side woke her up.

"Gabby, are you taking a break from sock searching?" Mr. Nuggy asked as he sat down and washed his face.

"I can't get any help. Did you look for my sock today?"

"No, I've been watching a bird, and I just got pushed out from my spot by Trunk. So now he's bird-watching and window-licking at the same time."

"Aren't you mad? I would have paw-popped him in the nose!"

"No, there is no time to be mad. I go with the flow. When one activity ends, I do something else." Mr. Nuggy squinted. "Maybe you should try going with the flow. Take a break from sock hunting and just allow your mind to rest. You know, when you can think clearly, the sock may just appear."

"Really? You believe that crap you're sprouting?"

"Gabby," Mr. Nuggy said as Gabby put her head on her paws.

"Well, when what you are doing is not working, but you keep doing it, they call that the sign of insanity. You can continue that way if you wish." He looked at her out of the corner of his eye.

He stretched. "I'm going to find another cushion to sit on. Just a reminder. When you hold on too tight to something, you can't hold on to anything else."

Gabby rolled her eyes and put her head back down.

An hour later, Gabby sat up, feeling sad about her sock.

Why can't I find it? Why won't any of the knuckleheads help me?

She stretched, gave herself a bath, and then let it go for the night. Something caught her eye as she walked to the PP Parlor.

Stopping short, she gasped.

"No, it can't be!"

Sticking out from behind the leg of the long table near the office was something white.

Her eyes locked on target. She walked in stealth mode, weaving around people and cats. At two feet from the table, she sprinted to the item.

Pawing at it furiously, she tried to extract it, but it was stuck behind the table leg. She didn't give up until a cat handler finally saw her and moved the table a bit.

The sock.

She spun around, tossed it in the air, bit it, and holding it tight, she rolled up to kick it with her back feet.

Trunk, who'd finished watching the bird, noticed Gabby and headed to Daisy.

"Daisy, Gabby found her sock."

"Thank the cat gods! She kept waking me up all day, disturbing my beauty sleep. I'm not getting any younger, so takes a lot of work to look this pretty," Daisy said, looking at Trunk for a reaction.

"She bothered me too. I missed sticking my paw in a coffee cup that had no lid. Do you know how rare that is?"

"Oh no, that's horrible." Daisy huffed.

"Are you teasing me?" Trunk asked.

"I just don't understand your motivation in life. You have it made here, but you do weird stuff."

"Judgmental much, Daisy?"

"You are so annoying. I should—"

"Hello," a deep voice said from behind Daisy.

In unison, Trunk and Daisy said, "Hello, Mr. Nuggy."

"I see Gabby found her sock. Did you congratulate her?" Trunk and Daisy put their heads down.

"No? Maybe you should. She was really upset yesterday."

Daisy hesitated but stood up. "Fine. I'll go grab Vee, separate her from that feather, and we'll talk to Gabby."

"Tell her congrats for me, Daisy. I got a coffee cup to stick my paw in."

"See, this is what I'm talking about! No wonder Gabby paw-pops you all the time." Daisy walked away, sticking her tail up. "You tell her yourself, Trunk. I'm not your secretary."

Mr. Nuggy closed his eyes and shook his head.

Trunk walked over to a young woman who was drinking her coffee on a side couch. He jumped up and, to her delight, he let her scratch his neck as he eyed her coffee. When she turned to talk to her friend, he stuck his paw in her coffee and licked it.

"Hey," the girl said and lifted the cup out of his way.

"They fall for it every time," Mr. Nuggy said as he went into the PP Parlor.

Gabby pranced around the Feline Foyer with her sock in her mouth. Daisy and Vee went up to her. She felt powerful. Accomplished. Pawing at the sock in the middle of the room, tossing it about, Gabby felt nothing could stop her. She'd found something everyone thought was impossible to find. Nothing could take her sock away.

The next moment, though, she was up in the air, sock in mouth, cocooned in Sarah's arms.

"What the hell?" she mumbled.

CHAPTER 25

Kit sat in her office, her feet on the desk. She removed her hand splint and wiggled her fingers around. The burn was healed, but the bruise was still present. As she looked at it, she couldn't believe it was all done in spite. She hated to think what she would have done to Marjorie a year ago when her own anger level was high. Although it was still bad, it wasn't half as bad as before.

Her phone rang. *Speaking of anger.*

"Yes. This is Kit Beck."

"Hi, Kitty, I am calling you as a favor to Judge Fink. You might not remember me, but I met you in the bathroom, of all places, at the courthouse a few weeks back. I gave you my card."

"The lipstick lady. I remember. You gave me advice in the bathroom. Weird, but whatever. You're calling for Judge Judy?"

"Her name is Judge Fink, not Judge Judy, and although 'the lipstick lady' is nice, I'm Ivy Tull."

"I still see you have your sense of humor, Ivy." Pausing, Kit continued. "I thought you were a lawyer. Why are you calling me unless I need one already? Someone else press charges or something?"

"No, just a follow-up regarding your case. Brenda Converse reached out. You have ignored two of her attempts to contact you."

"Oh. Did she tell you why? I broke my hand. There's been a murder and—"

"Kitty, I'm going to be frank. I don't care why you are missing the mandatory counseling. I'm just telling you to go. Judge Fink takes her orders seriously and will not tolerate a lack of follow-through."

You're just as pleasant, too, Kit thought.

"Although Kitty is nice, I'm Kit."

"O...K... Kit, you have one week to contact Brenda Converse, schedule a meeting, and go to it. Physically be in her office. I suggest you consider this as an olive branch. She won't extend it again. And last thing. If you cannot comply, you will be in contempt of a court order. Then you will need a lawyer. Understand?"

The throbbing in Kit's temples matched the throbbing in her hand. She was ready to scream.

"Um-hum," Kit said with force.

"Maybe one of these days, we can have a pleasant conversation. Goodbye, Kit." Ivy hung up.

Pressing the phone button hard, Kit wished she could slam it like she did as a kid. Instead, she kicked a box on the floor. It fell over, receipts flying everywhere. *Wonderful.*

There was a knock on the door. Sarah entered, holding Gabby.

"Here." She handed Gabby to Kit.

"Why are you handing me a cat?"

"I heard something fall and figured you either pushed it, kicked it, or something else. Figured you might need some therapeutic calming." She looked past the table. "Are you cleaning again? I see receipts all over the floor."

Kit ignored Sarah but looked at Gabby. "Your sock! Looks dingy, but I guess you found it."

Gabby jumped on the desk, dropped her sock, and leaned in to lick it.

"Does that human realize I was busy? She just picked me up and dropped me wherever she saw fit. I'm just a pawn in your game—" Gabby said but paused when she caught the scent of catnip.

Kit scratched her head.

"A missing sock? That dirty thing? We have brand new ones in the shop," Sarah said.

Gabby grabbed the sock in her mouth and jumped off the desk, but Kit caught her mid-flight.

"Hold on a second."

"Put me down," Gabby managed in a muffled voice.

"She's fast," Sarah said.

"I think this was a sock Nan gave her. It has a marking on the side."

"It looks like it needs a bath."

Gabby dropped the sock on the desk. "No, it doesn't. It;s fine. This is unacceptable."

"How do you know—?" Sarah said.

"I watch them. She's been looking all over the place; figured she was missing something." Kit picked up the sock while Gabby tried to paw it out of her hand. Kit held it higher.

"That's not fair. That's mine!"

"Hold on, Gabby." Looking closer, Kit noticed catnip stuck on the outside and a dark stain across the side of the sock.

"Give that back to me. Get your own damn sock!"

"Gabby, I'm sorry, girl. I'm gonna have to borrow this for a few," Kit said as she rubbed Gabby under her chin.

"No! I've been looking for it for days. You can't have it." A loud howl pierced the room.

Sarah was startled. "Wow. She's not happy."

"True."

"I can get her another one," Sarah said, turning to walk out.

"Don't bother. She only wants this one." Kit nodded her head to the left of the door. "I tried two other socks the other night."

Kit kissed Gabby on the head. "Sorry, girl. I'll get it back as soon as I can."

"I'll never forgive you," Gabby said. She jumped off the desk and ran out of the office.

"Are you going to tell me what's so special about that toy?" Sarah asked.

"I can't put my finger on it, but I will."

Sarah pointed at Kit's hand. "Try another finger."

"Okay, Miss Comedienne," Kit said. She tossed her hand wrap at Sarah.

CHAPTER 26

Every time she went to the office, Kit stared at the cat toy in the plastic bag.

She spun in her office chair to look out the window into the Feline Foyer. A cat played with patrons; another jumped to catch a feather. And there was Trunk, sprawled out in front of a little boy who was squealing with delight. Laughter and fun happened here. Well, except for Gabby. She had sulked all day and wouldn't talk to Kit at all.

Nan did good, she thought. *Despite all the crap that's happened this past week, this place is pawesome. You didn't say that, Kit.*

She spun back around and began twirling her hair. Surveying the desk, she realized the paperwork was overwhelming.

At least the books for the past week have been done. They did lose money being closed Sunday and Monday, but they could make it up fairly quickly.

Kit opened her office door to listen and caught a whiff of baked cookies as the door from the kitchen opened. Janice walked by her office.

Janice was usually spot-on, focused, and motivated. Today she seemed jumpy and distracted, even getting irritated when a cat was in the way.

"Janice." Kit leaned back in the chair to catch her attention in the doorway.

"Yeah?"

"Do you have a minute?"

Janice took off her plastic gloves, wiping her hands on her smock.

"What's up?" She didn't make eye contact. "I can't stay long. I have a tray in the oven. I'm not supposed to leave it—"

"It's only for a minute."

"Alright."

"I'm going to get right to the point."

Janice started shifting her weight.

Kit leaned back toward the desk, pulled out a folder, and held up a Post-it note for Janice to look at.

Janice looked away.

"You recognize it? Your handwriting?"

She remained silent.

"It says, 'Leave me out of this.' I know it's your handwriting."

Janice sat on the arm of the couch, looking down. A tear fell from her eye. In a soft voice, she said, "Marjorie was blackmailing Craig."

"What! Why?"

As she spoke, she seemed almost relieved. "She found out he was stealing some of the high-end cat food from his employer to make the cat cookies he sells here. She's been getting the cookies for a steal."

Kit rocked in her office chair. "How did she find out?"

"We were talking in the hallway. We didn't know she was in the break room doing the books." Janice slumped. "The cat door creates an echo chamber when it's open. She heard everything."

"Cat door?"

"Before we built the PP Parlor, we used the break room for the cats," Janice said.

"What did she hear?" Kit asked.

"We were talking about him working at the warehouse, and I told him it was stupid to take the cat food. By the time she found out, he had already received a down payment for the cat cookies. She then refused to give him the rest. When I found out what she was doing, I was so mad. I wrote that note to tell her I was done being used to get at Craig.

She laughed at me. I... like Craig; he's a good guy. He works so hard to make these cookies. They're his special recipe. He does all the research and even talks to a veterinarian to make sure they're good for the cats."

"He was stealing."

"He wasn't really stealing. He was taking the bags that were damaged that were going to get tossed out, but then he thought she was going to order a lot, so he needed more, and there were no more damaged bags, so he broke into a few."

"Why didn't you tell me this at the apartment? You threw him under the bus," Kit asked.

"I wasn't trying to. I really didn't want to get him in trouble. Everyone is going to think he killed her."

Kit exhaled loudly. "You can get back to work."

Janice didn't move. "Are you going to the police?"

"Yes."

Janice started talking fast. "But you can't. I mean, Craig will get in trouble. I'll get in trouble for lying."

"I don't know, but I have to tell them. There was a murder here. I don't have a choice."

"Am I...fired?"

Kit tapped her pen and faced Janice.

"No, but I need to trust you. Next time, tell me the truth."

Janice started crying. "Thanks, Kit."

As she walked out, Kit noticed something was off, but what? Maybe Janice's fondness for Craig was more than she was telling.

CHAPTER 27

Still working on the budget, Kit took a break to enjoy a coffee and a walk around to meet people. For the first time since she arrived, she felt somewhat normal. She'd been in the office for too long; cleaning and going through every box. Marjorie had made a mess and left it for the staff.

She even learned to make a cappuccino. No one offered to try it. Lucky for her. She decided the best for everyone was if she stuck to her plain coffee in her own coffeepot.

Sarah was amazing in the café. She engaged with customers and staff with ease. She was patient with Kit, but also made sure she did things by the book. After Kit's training, they got the office cleaned out, and Kit gave her Marjorie's set of keys. Now it was Kit and Sarah's office.

Much better roommate, she thought.

For a few moments, they sat in silence, taking in all the work they'd done. Kit thought how her life had changed in such a short time and how the energy here was so much better without Marjorie around. Sad but true.

They rearranged the storage room to make space for boxes from the office, then brainstormed how to make their office better. Marjorie had been a slob. Literally. She had left catnip and crumbs under her table, along with a few unidentified packages of who knows what.

Sarah mentioned that Marjorie loved to drop loose catnip on the floor of the office for the cats. The problem was she never vacuumed it up.

Kit and Sarah headed to the PP Parlor to hang out for a bit while Brian got supplies to expand the cat door for Trunk.

Kit watched the cats who were cuddled in the cubbyhole. An orange tabby sounded muffled as the gray cat meowed a bit. She wondered if they knew her ability. It always surprised her how she could hear some very clearly, but others sounded garbled or like a backward record. A few, like Trunk, only had one or a few words to say.

Sarah and Kit cleaned cat boxes. In mid-scoop, Kit said under her breath, "Some career goals. And damn, these cats really sh—"

The back door slammed as Brian walked in. "Oh, you got the box that Vee uses. Stinky."

Kit turned toward Sarah, who was giggling. "Sarah?"

"Hey, everyone gets christened by Vee. You're not part of the team until you smelled that cat box up close."

Sarah went with Brian to his desk to go over paperwork.

Kit got up slowly, feeling the strain in her back and the ache in her hand. She noticed Craig at the door.

"Hey, Kit, I didn't know you would be here," he said. "I made the cat treats you asked for. Twelve boxes."

"Wow, you're fast," Kit said.

"Been up all night. Where do you want me to put them?" he said, twisting his dolly toward her.

Kit eyed the packages. "These look great! What price did Marjorie give you again?"

Craig paused. "Um. I need to look at my receipt. Um. She didn't give me a final price. I got a down payment."

"Craig, can we talk for a minute?"

Craig looked around and found a chair with a cushion covered in white fur. He sat down rather quickly.

Kit pulled another chair closer and sat. He moved back.

"I found Marjorie's receipts for your cat cookies."

Nodding. "Yes, the down payment."

"Well, yes and no."

Craig leaned forward. "She told me—"

"Just a minute. Let me finish. Marjorie always put a code on every vendor deposit slip she created. It was her way of knowing she had more to pay. It looked like she was only planning on giving you the deposit money and nothing else. Is that true?"

He shook his foot. "Yeah, she only paid me a quarter of what she told me she would, and that's the amount I used to make the product," he said.

"Craig, why didn't you say anything?"

"To who? I didn't know who to talk to."

"I have another question," Kit said. "Was she blackmailing you?"

"Blackmail? No."

"Huh." Kit rubbed her face. "Because I have someone who swears that she was blackmailing you so she wouldn't have to pay, and she did this because you were borrowing cat food at your other job."

Craig's eyes got wide, and his face red.

"Craig, did you kill her to keep her quiet about the blackmail?" Kit asked.

Craig jumped up so fast the chair slammed against the wall, tipping over. He lunged toward her, inches away from her face.

"I didn't kill her!" he said, his hot breath hitting her face.

Kit moved her chair back and stood up slowly. "Craig, it's only a question."

"I didn't frigging kill her." He bent down and grabbed his chair.

Brian moved toward Kit, but she held up a hand. He stopped.

"Craig," she said in a shaky voice.

"Who told you about the cat food?" he asked, this time his voice softer.

"It doesn't matter."

Picking his chair up, he dropped onto it. "It does to me. I can't believe you think I would kill her! Did I hate that bitch? Yes, everyone did. Damn it!" He ran his fingers through his hair, leaving a clump standing upright.

"Yeah, alright, I was taking the food, but I told my manager right after Marjorie died. I said nothing because of this reason, right here." He blew out his breath and stood back up. "My manager told me if I pay wholesale, I can use the food. I paid the money back!"

Kit felt her body sink. "Oh."

"Damn it!" Craig said, pacing back and forth.

Brian moved closer to Kit. "Let's just calm down."

"Don't tell me to calm down!" Craig shouted, then realized it was Brian talking.

"Sorry, man."

He walked out; cat fur stuck to his butt.

As the door slammed, Sarah walked over.

"What was that about?"

Kit's hands shook. "I asked Craig about the deposits, the blackmail, and if he killed Marjorie."

"Blackmail?"

Kit filled Sarah in on her conversation with Janice.

Brian shook his head as he moved Craig's dolly and boxes of cookies off to the side of the room.

"I don't know why you're asking these questions. What if he was the murderer, Kit?" he asked.

"I dunno."

"He was scary. I'm surprised you didn't throw cat litter at him or flip out on him," Sarah said.

"I didn't expect his reaction. It startled me," Kit said, noticing her legs were still shaking. "Sarah, do me a favor. Go to the office and grab Gabby's sock from the desk. It's in a ziplock bag. "

"Sure, what's going on?"

"I have a hunch. Don't take it out of the bag," she said as Sarah left.

"What's going on, Kit?" Brian asked.

She walked over to the dolly and inspected it. There were twelve boxes of cat cookies with three dozen in each. So much work. Kit could feel her heart sink. Such a great presentation, and to finish it all in a few days. She leaned down and moved the dolly back and forth.

Sarah entered and handed the bag to Kit.

She moved the bag left and right, turning it over. "Look!"

Sarah leaned over Kit's shoulder. "What am I looking at?"

"The dolly wheels made this mark on Gabby's sock."

"Okay. . . I don't get it." Sarah stood back up.

Kit stood up with the help of Sarah. "There's catnip and what looks like blood on the sock."

"He rolled over it, so?" Sarah said.

"How is there blood if she wasn't dead when he left?" Kit asked.

Sarah's face paled. She put her hand to her mouth. "Oh. My. God. Did he kill her?" She looked at Brian.

She ran to the back door and locked it. "What if he comes back for his dolly?"

"I don't think he's coming back, but just in case, you need to call the police and stay out of this," Brian said.

"I'm surprised you aren't more interested. You watch a lot of Hallmark Channel movies," Sarah said, tipping her head toward Brian.

Brian dropped his hands. "TV, not real life. Screw that. I'm not feeling the desire to be stabbed."

Sarah smiled.

"I'll call the detective now," Kit said. Her hands shook for the second time that day.

CHAPTER 28

T he detective entered the cat café about twenty minutes later. He grabbed a coffee and banged like a madman on the door to the Feline Foyer.

"Really? You couldn't ring the bell?" Kit said as she let him in.

Standing in her office, she told him about the conversation with Janice and then the discussion, or confrontation with Craig. He spoke his mind about her being involved but listened as she told him about the blackmail and the dolly and the wheel mark she saw. She also told him to touch base with Sarah because she had seen Marjorie and Craig argue.

He stomped around her office. "Your name is not Detective Kitty."

"You're right, it's Kit. Detective Kitty sounds like a porn name. But Detective Kit sounds better than Detective Flowers or Detective Seaweed."

"Seriously?" he said in a high-pitched voice.

She shrugged her shoulders.

He took the bag with the sock, the Post-it note, and the receipts, and had his officer take the dolly with the cat cookies.

As he left the room, she threw a stuffed mouse that squeaked when it bounced off his head. She laughed.

He looked back in disbelief. "Seriously?"

"You need to level up your vocabulary. You just said that."

He left, trying not to smile.

She shouted at him. "I want my cat cookies back when you're done. They aren't Girl Scout cookies. You're welcome, Detective Seaweed."

"No problem, Kitty."

Cracking a smile, she dug through her purse, and pulled out her phone to scroll for a number. A number she'd been dreading calling. Spinning her hair between her fingers, she gazed at the name. Pursing her lips, she held her breath as the answering machine picked up.

"Yes, this is Kitty Beck. I want to make an appointment for my mandatory sessions. You can call me—"

Beep.

"Great! Clear your friggin' in-box!" She hurled her phone onto the couch.

"Wow, you really need to work on your anger issues," Gabby said, standing in the doorway. "Where's my sock?"

"I have anger issues? You're yelling at me. Cat calling the kettle black, I see," Kit said.

Gabby popped up on the couch with ease and turned toward Kit. She meowed.

"That's cute, but your sock is not here."

"Where is my sock?"

"The detective took it."

CHAPTER 29

"He's a person of interest," he said.

Moving the phone away from her ear, she shivered at the thought.

She shouted at the detective. "I can't believe he would do it. He looked right into my eyes the other day. He looked like an innocent child."

"Why are you surprised, Kit? You brought all the evidence to me, and you tried to knock me over with it, including attempting to knock me over with a squeaky mouse. We picked him up this morning for questioning."

"What did he say?" she asked.

"That he's innocent. We're having the sock tested and going over his timeline, but so far, he's looking good for this. Janice came in for another talk regarding the blackmailing."

Kit slumped into the chair.

"I didn't mean to give you hell yesterday, but you can't go asking questions like that," he said. She heard him shift papers.

"Will I get my sock and cookies back?" She could hear mumbling on the phone as if he had his hand over it.

"Well?" she asked.

"Those items are part of the case, so it's doubtful."

"He didn't have the cookies with him. He used the dolly to drop off supplies, then probably wheeled it over there with his samples," Kit said.

"There could be trace evidence on it. Besides, I'm going to hand them out as treats for my officers."

"I thought cops liked doughnuts, not cat cookies. They are edible, you know. Charge extra for each box. It'll pay for the mess you made in my shop."

"Wow, you have no sense of humor today."

"You had no sense of humor yesterday, so we're even." She let out a big breath. "This has been rough on my staff, and I hate to tell them about this until I know for sure. Part of me is relieved, but another part, my intuition, thinks he is innocent."

"You told me he lunged at you in the piddle parlor."

Kit twisted her hair hard. "It's PP Parlor, and yeah, he did, but he looked more hurt and disappointed than angry. And I know angry."

"Well, the facts tell the tale," he said.

"Are you making a cat joke?"

"I thought it was funny. Again, no sense of humor today."

"The sock. I really need the sock back. I have an angry seven-pound cat who is not happy that you took her toy."

"Give her a new one from the shop," the detective said.

"You really don't understand cats. She was looking all over for that sock. She found it, and I took it away."

"The cat will get over it."

"First off, the cat is Gabby, the cat who was in the break room playing with the knife. Second, she will not get over it."

He chuckled. "I remember her. She's a little spitfire. She scared my techs when they had to take a sample of her fur."

"I will send her after you if you don't return her sock."

With a hint of sarcasm in his voice, he said, "That is more terrifying than murder. I'll see what I can do."

The Feline Foyer seemed eerie. Kit peeked her head out of the office door. Everyone sat still, spread out among a few tables. Even the cats were quiet.

"Why are you sitting out here? We're supposed to meet in the break room."

She heard a bunch of mumbling and heads turned, but no one spoke.

Finally, Brian said, "No one wants to use that room anymore."

"Okay, I get it. But we can't meet here. Not while there are patrons in the building. Let's go out back to the picnic tables," Kit said.

"Is everything alright?" Sarah asked as she met up with Kit.

"Craig is a person of interest."

Sarah gasped. "We were right." She and Kit stepped aside, letting others walk by them.

"I feel kind of weird about it. Honestly, I think he's innocent."

Sarah and Kit walked out into the sun. "Really? I'm surprised. He was so angry, and he had blood on his dolly."

"Allegedly, it's blood. They haven't tested it. I told the detective that he looked more disappointed than angry."

Walking to the patio, the rocks crunched beneath her feet. The area was small, but it held two long picnic tables with a huge tarp covering both. The voices grew louder as everyone settled.

"Hey," Kit called out. The talking stopped, and she leaned back on her heels. "Earlier today, I got a call from Detective Flowers. Craig is now a person of interest."

She heard a loud gasp from Janice as she sank onto a bench shouting, "No!"

Peter leaned down to support her.

Janice cried, "He didn't do this."

"Why would he kill her?" one server asked from the other table. "He seems so nice."

"He's just a person of interest. Not arrested yet."

"Besides, nice doesn't mean you can't kill someone. Look at all those serial killers who are really nice," another kid in the back chimed in.

"Yeah," Peter said, looking at Kit, then back at Janice. "Even Kit has anger issues, but she's nice."

Kit glared at him, not sure what to say.

"Peter," Brian said.

"Well, it's true. Craig wouldn't do this. He's too chill," Peter said.

"This is hard for all of us, so let's just wait and see what happens," Kit said.

"They're still processing things, right, Kit?" Brian said in a soft tone.

"Yes, that's true."

Peter spoke up. "Can I take Janice home? She can't work like this."

Kit looked over at Sarah.

Sarah nodded. "Yeah, I have another cook who can finish up."

"Come back, Peter. We have a cat door to finish," Brian said.

Peter began walking with Janice leaning on his arm the whole time.

Leanne appeared and bounced over to the picnic tables, her hair now white.

"What's going on?" she asked.

Peter spun around. "Why are you back here? This is a staff meeting. Besides, it's none of your business."

Kit put her hand to her mouth. Brian touched her shoulder and looked at Leanne. He whispered to Kit. "I got this."

He walked toward Peter.

Kit put her hand on Leanne, apologized for Peter, and told her what was going on as Sarah finished up the meeting. Peter helped Janice into the front seat of the car as Brian leaned down. Kit could see Peter nod as Brian spoke. A few times it looked like he shot daggers at her. The hair on the back of her neck stood up, and she felt a full-body chill.

What did I do to this kid?

Brian returned to Sarah and Kit, who were still at the table. "You could have given me a heads-up."

"Damn, I'm sorry, Brian. I got the call earlier today."

"I don't believe it. Craig is a good guy," Brian said.

"Yeah, everyone says that."

"How about Peter? He was looking at Kit like he wanted to stab her. Creepy," Sarah said.

"You saw that? It gave me goose bumps."

Brian looked back at Peter's van, which was pulling away. "Peter's a kid, and he liked Marjorie. This has been hard on him. He speaks his mind even when it's inappropriate."

"Sounds like someone else we know, or should say knew. Marjorie spoke her mind too," Sarah said.

Kit watched Leanne bounce away with another staff member. Pointing at Leanne, Kit said, "She has no boundaries. You would think they'd get along."

"Marjorie hated Leanne, so Peter hates her too." Brian's voice was sad.

Kit just sighed.

"We should get some answers in a day," Brian said.

"How do you know that?" Kit asked.

"I watch a lot of murder mysteries," he said as he headed to the back door of the PP Parlor.

"Cozy mysteries. He watches cozy mysteries," Sarah said with a giggle.

CHAPTER 30

The atmosphere at the cat café changed. It felt like the staff was all in individual bubbles. They were friendly serving customers, but in their own world. It always struck Kit as odd how some people fell apart while others around them bitched because they were missing one drop of milk in their latte.

They all needed the distraction the day brought but also wanted to go home and put their heads on their pillows. There were a lot of cats getting hugged in the PP Parlor. Brian had never had so much company as he had this week. Not that he complained.

Vee was in her glory, but Gabby sulked around, and since Kit was the one who took her favorite toy, she refused to talk to her. *You would think it would be no big deal, but when you communicate with someone and they stop talking, it's uncomfortable.*

Sarah wanted to know the best way to help her servers during this difficult time. None of them were therapists, so the question was difficult to answer.

"When are you going to see your counselor?"

"I have to be there by seven," Kit said.

"Ask her how to handle this. I'm at a loss."

"Alright."

"I'm gonna finish up petty cash. Marjorie left cleaning to do. I'd rather stay busy than go home." Sarah looked around the office, appearing more defeated by the minute.

"Are you sure you don't want to head home? It's been a long day, and you look exhausted."

"Nah. It'll be nice to have a place to finish my paperwork for a change. People love to chat with me, and the cats love to pester me. Not that I mind the cats."

"Well, you're easy to talk with, so I can see why." Kit could tell Sarah's smile was forced. "I'm surprised Marjorie didn't plan for you and Brian. She should have given you a better space. I mean, this office is enormous!"

"Brian likes his office in the back room. He's great with people, but he enjoys being with the cats more," Sarah said.

"Before I leave, let's go hug a cat. We have the best jobs, right?" Kit said.

They headed for the PP Parlor. The café was almost empty, just a couple talking in the far corner and a kid on a computer. In the Feline Foyer, a few people milled about, trying to catch a cat or find one that would enjoy serious petting. Kit listened, but she heard nothing, just a few whirls and purrs.

In the parlor, they each coaxed a cat out of a cubbyhole and into a hug. Sarah held the small gray cat, who cooed as he bumped her head. She looked like she was about to cry. She pushed her face deep into its fur. Kit found a fluffy orange cat who sounded like he was talking backward. This was perfect because she couldn't deal with chitchat right now. She inhaled deeply. Nothing like the warmth and smell of a cat.

"Good idea," Sarah said in a muted voice.

"Someone I know told me it's excellent therapy," Kit said.

A few more hugs, pets, and sniffs, and they both put the cats down, wiping fur off their clothing and waving flying hairs away from their faces. Kit looked at Brian's desk.

"Not for nothing are all these chairs covered in cat fur." Kit laughed.

Sarah read a bulletin board and picked up the evening paper. "That's why they wear light brown khakis. Can you imagine if they didn't?"

"Did you see all the cat fur on Craig's butt the other day?" Kit said, suppressing a chuckle.

Sarah nodded, flipping through the paper. "He looked like he sat on one and killed it. If anyone saw him, they would think he murdered cats too."

Kit bumped Sarah with her arm. "Sarah. When did you become so snarky?"

"I'll deny it." Sarah laughed, but quickly turned a sad face.

"I have proof. The cats heard you, too," Kit said.

"Luckily, cats can't talk," she said, barely paying attention.

Kit turned away to hide her expression. Sarah still didn't know, and Kit didn't think she could handle another bombshell well, even though it would be perfect timing otherwise.

Looking back at Kit, Sarah asked, "Hey, did you read the paper today?"

"No, why?"

Sarah read out loud. "'Saturday Night Murder at the Cat Café.' They even have a picture of you."

"Me? Let me see." Kit looked over Sarah's shoulder.

"You have your finger up the detective's nose." Sarah laughed hard.

"That's a terrible picture. I was pointing, but I wasn't that close."

"Pictures don't lie." Sarah continued on. "That's not the best of it. They interviewed a woman who said, 'All my friends are calling the murder the Caturday Knife Special.' Leave it to a cat purr-son to come up with that."

"Oh no, you just didn't," Kit said.

"I did." She hit Kit on the arm with the paper.

"What was that, anyway? A movie?"

"Yeah. A movie about a murderer and I think there was a song too. Way before my time." Sarah left the PP Parlor.

Kit left ten minutes later. She found Trunk in the hallway, sitting in front of the break room.

Pawing at the door, he kept saying, "Sit. Sit. Sit."

Kit leaned over and petted his head. "Sorry, fella, you can't go in there right now."

As she passed the break room door, she felt a chill go up her spine.

CHAPTER 31

S itting on an overstuffed couch that felt like a large marshmallow, Kit twirled her hair. The doctor's office waiting room was kind of cozy. There was a salt lamp in the corner and a tall lamp with beads on a coffee table next to her. The rug had a multicolored pattern. Provided you didn't have a history of seizures, you were all set.

The yellow door to the office opened. A woman in her forties with long brown hair and light-green eyes extended her hand. Her voice was soft, and she had a gentle smile.

"Hello, Kit. I'm Brenda Converse."

Kit nodded and shook her hand.

Brenda moved back from the door as Kit entered. The same rug in the waiting room extended into her office, but a large light-brown throw rug offset the busyness. In front of two windows was a short bookshelf with a minimal number of books, plants in all shapes and sizes, plus a few crystals, candles, and other items worth displaying. Next to that bookshelf was a leather chair, and on the opposite side were two loveseats. The windows were open, so a gentle breeze caught Brenda's hair.

As she brushed it away from her face, she nodded to the loveseat that Kit was to sit on.

Kit kept twirling her hair as Brenda looked down at her folder and pad of paper.

"Let me get this off my chest. You called the judge on me?"

"Yes," Brenda said without missing a beat.

"That's it, just yes?" She'd expected an explanation.

"Yes." Brenda leaned back in her chair and crossed her legs. "If you're looking for an apology, you will not get one. They mandated you to attend these sessions." She placed her hands in her lap. "You can work with me or someone else, but you must attend."

"This is bullshit."

"I appreciate you being direct with your question, so I will return that courtesy and be direct with my answer." She looked directly at Kit. "Why do you think this is bullshit?"

"I don't see how talking about this is going to help," Kit said, adjusting herself on the sofa.

"What do you think will help?" Brenda asked.

"Isn't it your job to tell me?"

Brenda began talking with her hands. "Let me get this straight. You say this is bullshit, but you won't tell me what I can do to help, and you also expect me to do my job and help you. Did I get that right?"

"That statement right there is why people have anger issues," Kit said.

"People? Meaning you?"

"I guess I'm the people. You really want me to tell you all about my life, my feelings, my issues, the good and bad parts of my life, blah, blah?"

"Yes."

"A woman of many words," Kit said.

"Let's start with what happened in California." She looked at Kit as if she were the only person on the planet. It was unnerving, yet Kit felt that she really wanted to know.

Kit told the story about the couple on the running path.

"He ended up getting his skate stuck in a grate and broke his arm." Kit rolled her eyes.

"You find this situation annoying?" Brenda asked.

"Yes, I do. He acted like he was doing me a favor by not suing me."

"Kit, he did do you a favor. That could have cost thousands of dollars."

Kit rubbed her hands together. "I had to apologize to him and his wife. That was rough. I wanted to push him again." She felt nothing but irritation. "Are you going to tell me what a bad person I am and how I should be nicer?"

"No. Actions have consequences, which you're paying for right now. Your time, your energy, and your money. I am not cheap." Brenda smiled.

She glanced at her papers. "I see you received twelve sessions with me. That's excessive. Most only get eight." She whistled. "You upset the judge, didn't you?"

Kit just sat there.

"How did you end up in Massachusetts when this case was in California?"

"I grew up here in Misty Bottom. My grandmother took care of me and my sister after my mom died."

"I'm sorry to hear that. Do you get along with your sister?" Brenda asked as she made a note on her pad.

"Oh yeah, we were best friends growing up. Just, I haven't seen her in a while."

"What's her name?"

"Sky."

"Pretty name. And your grandmother's name?"

Kit's eyes lit up. "Her name is Victoria, but everyone calls her Nan. She hates Grandma or Nana. Even the people at the cat café call her Nan."

"Do you talk to your grandmother?" Brenda asked.

"We talk frequently over Zoom or on the phone. Haven't seen her in person in a while. Now she's on a cruise for six months. She knew I was heading back, so she offered me a job running the cat café and taking over her apartment in the back." Kit bit her nails.

"That's an enormous responsibility."

"Yup. I have a master's degree in business management."

"But?" Brenda said in a flat tone.

"But what?"

"You look uncomfortable about it."

"I don't know if she went on her cruise to give me the job or if she was lucky that I mucked up so I could take over the job. She didn't tell me the size of the café, either."

"Does it matter?"

"Well, yeah! I don't want to be the one child who needs fixing and helping."

"Kit, we all need fixing and helping," Brenda said, using air quotes. "We are all in this thing called life together."

"Wow, that's so Hallmark," Kit said.

"Thank you. I have my moments."

Kit turned on the loveseat to look out the big window. The breeze felt wonderful on her face.

"Tell me about your other job. Um. The warehouse job," Brenda said.

Kit felt her face flush. "No."

"No?"

"You can add being a parrot to your job description. I would rather not discuss that right now."

"Okay. We can table it for another time. Tell me how you felt when you found out about the size of the café."

"I was mad. Wouldn't you be? I thought it was a tiny café with a barista and a cat. Not thirty employees and fifteen cats, plus a murder and a partridge in a pear tree. She knew I would have said no."

"You would have for sure?"

"Yup. I wanted to come back this way to simplify my life."

"How has it been going so far?"

"I lost my shit in the parking lot the first day. All the employees watched me have a tantrum."

"At least it's out in the open."

Kit spun back around to look at Brenda. "Why is that a good thing?"

Brenda put her pen down. "We'll get into anger and why it happens, but for now, support is a good thing."

"I don't want people walking on eggshells around me."

"Are they?" Brenda asked.

"Um, it doesn't seem like it, but with the murder, we're all out of sorts."

"Tell me about the murder."

Kit leaned her head back and told Brenda about Marjorie and the boxes of litter, her hand, the cats covered in blood, the dead body, the clues, Craig, Janice, and everything else. She talked for a long time.

"This is a lot to process for you. How many outbursts have you had since you got here?"

Kit twisted her hair. "I dunno, about half a dozen."

"That's not bad, considering the stress you're under. Just moving across the states is stressful enough."

"Yeah, it's a lot of stress for my employees. Oh, one of my supervisors wants to know how to help her staff."

"It's a lot of stress for you too. Let's not forget that you are part of this team," Brenda said. "As for your supervisor, just tell her to listen."

"Really? That's your wisdom?"

"Yes."

Kit ran her hands over her face getting a whiff of the bandage on her hand. "What is up with the one-word answers?"

"Kit, I keep things simple. Tell me about Marjorie. You mentioned your grandmother liked her?"

"My grandmother sees the best in people. Even Sarah, who sees the best in people, saw that Marjorie was a bit—...um..."

"You can say bitch. I don't care about swearing. Please speak freely."

"She was more than a bitch."

"Okay, go on."

"I was planning on firing her on Monday, but she went and got murdered Saturday night."

"I saw the newspaper." Brenda nodded. "Do you feel guilty about wanting to fire her?"

"No."

Brenda tipped her pen toward Kit and smiled.

"You ask a lot of questions. Can't you just help me get rid of this issue?"

"No."

"Should of seen that coming. Seriously, that is getting old."

"Okay," Brenda said as Kit looked up, gritting her teeth. "I am making a point. You can talk to someone. You can be direct, and you can do it without blowing a gasket. A simple yes or no works great."

"That is your advice? Seems too simple."

"Let me ask you this. How would you reprimand a cat if it was getting into trouble?" Brenda asked.

"I would tell them no."

Brenda spread her hands out and smiled.

"I'm not a cat!"

"Humans aren't much different. A man wrote a book about training dogs, and women used it to train their husbands. It worked. Alright, it's time to wrap up for today. I want you to use yes and no more often. I want to see you this coming Friday."

"That's in two days. Why so soon?"

"You are going through a lot of changes right now, plus we have the extra sessions," Brenda said.

"Geez, thanks."

"Oh, Kit. One more thing?"

"Yeah?" Kit said, getting up to stretch.

"I saw your picture in the paper. Why did you put your finger up the detective's nose?"

Kit dropped her arms down fast as Brenda held back a chuckle.

CHAPTER 32

Sarah called Kit in a panic. She had worked on the petty cash after Kit left and discovered some discrepancies, including missing money. Exhaustion from her session made it impossible to concentrate, so Kit said they'd work on it the next day.

Kit shuddered at the thought of eleven more sessions. It wasn't bad, but that woman was odd, and the one-word answers were annoying. Kit changed into her pjs to enjoy a night on the couch with popcorn, a blanket, and a good movie. Her favorite type of night.

"No murder mysteries, Kit," she said out loud.

She made popcorn, doing it the old-fashioned way with Nan's air popper. Plopping on the couch, she scanned the movie list. Romance. *Perfect*, she thought, tossing a piece of popcorn in her mouth.

A banging noise at her door startled her.

She put the TV on pause and listened. A murderer at her door was her first thought, even though she realized most murderers wouldn't knock.

Bang!

A soft meow echoed in the hallway, and Kit finally exhaled. *That's better.*

Jumping off the couch, she opened the door, and Gabby scampered in, her tail and nose in the air.

"Hello to you too, Miss Gabby."

She pranced around, smelling the couch, the carpet, and back to Kit. She rubbed against Kit's leg and stopped.

Kit looked down at her tiny body, piglet-sized feet, and big saucer eyes. She was adorable. It was enough to melt the hardest of hearts.

"Yes, Gabby?"

She meowed.

"You weren't talking to me yesterday, so if you want to, start now. I don't understand 'meow.'"

"Did you get my sock back yet?"

Kit hopped back on the couch and tucked her feet under the blanket. Grabbing the popcorn, she turned the TV on to start the movie.

"No. The detective is still processing it."

Gabby leaped on her coffee table and stood there in front of Kit's face.

Kit sighed and put the TV on pause again. "Gabby. I don't have your sock. It's out of my hands, but I told the detective you want it back. Please move; you're blocking my view." Kit tried to look around Gabby.

"I need my sock," she hissed.

"And I need to relax. It's been a tough week." Kit looked directly at Gabby. "Can you move?"

Gabby lowered her eyes into tiny slits. "This is unacceptable. I want a lawyer."

Kit dropped her feet to the floor and laughed as popcorn bounced onto the blanket. "Do you know what a lawyer is?"

"Yes, it's a human who carries a briefcase and can get my sock back."

"Lawyers are expensive. How are you going to pay for one?"

"Look at this face. I'm not paying. A few cuddles and purrs and I can hire the best lawyer in town."

"I know a woman, but she's in California. I don't think your charm would work with her."

Gabby tipped her head. Kit realized arguing with her was ridiculous. This was a no-win situation.

"Something smells good." Gabby jumped onto the couch, snagged a piece of popcorn that was on the blanket, and jumped back to the floor.

"Hey!" Kit said as she heard crunching by her feet. "Popcorn is not for cats."

"That's good because it tastes like cardboard," she said, washing her face.

"Right, coming from a cat who licks her ass and eats mice."

"Hey! I don't eat mice! I am not that kind of cat."

Gabby hopped back onto the coffee table. "I'm gonna be down eight lives by the time I get my sock back. You need to make some phone calls." She leaned in closer to Kit.

"I did. There is nothing I can do right now. Can you please move?"

Kit lifted her leg to the couch. Gabby nipped her on the shin.

"Ouch! What did you do that for?" Kit rubbed her shin, realizing it had been more of a surprise than painful. Gabby hadn't even broken skin.

"You taste like cardboard too." Gabby stuck her tongue out and made a coughing sound.

Kit rolled her eyes. "Oh, the drama!"

"I'm mad at you," Gabby said, turning her back toward Kit.

"Okay. Are you going to watch this movie with me?"

"No." She walked to the door and meowed.

Kit climbed off the couch one more time to open the door.

"Good night, Gabby."

"Whatever. Oh, shave your legs. Your stubble scratched my chin."

Her tail twitched as she walked away.

CHAPTER 33

"What did you watch?" Sarah asked, rubbing the sleep from her eyes.

"Some romantic comedy. I fell asleep halfway through it."

Sarah wrapped her hands around her coffee. "Yeah, I'm exhausted too." She took a sip and then gazed into the mug. "I couldn't stop thinking about that missing money."

"I called the detective; don't freak until we find out what they took that was in the cash register."

They stood near the office door watching Leanne, who sat in the middle of the foyer with Peanut Butter.

"Who's a-a good b-boy?" She leaned over and let her hair, still white, fall over his fur. Peanut Butter rolled around.

"Oh, she's going to get clawed in the nose," Kit said.

"Nah, not Peanut Butter. He loves her," Sarah said as she tapped Kit on the arm. She tipped her head toward the café door.

Detective Flowers walked in, holding a big paper bag. He noticed Leanne and frowned.

"Wasn't her hair blue?" he asked.

"It was. Did you bring us breakfast?"

"Nope. Something better."

"What can be better than bacon?"

He smiled.

"The cat sock?"

"Why is that damn sock so important?"

"I told you already. The cat is angry and wants her sock back. I think she's going to sue you," Kit said.

"Well, here's your money tray. Lawyers are expensive," the detective said as Sarah took the tray into the office.

"I told her the same thing," Kit said.

The detective shook his head. "Your receipts are in there too. You had a lot of money in the register."

"We were hoping you got my message."

"Marjorie only did petty cash once a month. Everyone uses debit cards nowadays. Sarah, what was the number we came up with yesterday?"

"Um. Let me look. Nine thousand, two hundred," she shouted from the office.

Kit looked at the police receipt and frowned. "There's only four thousand two hundred in here. Did you buy doughnuts with our money, detective? We're off five thousand."

"What?"

"Sarah did the books, and the total was nine thousand, two hundred."

"You make nine grand a month in petty cash in this place?" he asked.

"That's what you're focusing on in this conversation?" Kit asked.

"Well, yeah."

"More than that, detective. You've tasted our coffee, right? Do you think Craig stole the money?" Sarah asked.

"Why would he leave all *this* money? The money from the register was right there. But the money bag was an easy grab?" Kit said.

"I'll talk to him about it. We'll talk later, Kitty."

"It's Kit, Detective Seaweed."

He walked around Leanne, heading to the café to grab a coffee.

"Tell them the coffee is on us," Sarah said.

He waved.

"That was nice of you, Sarah."

"We need him on our side. He likes to tease you, huh?"

The barista serving the detective eyed Kit from beyond the window. Kit nodded and waited for him to take the first sip. Detective Flowers seemed to nod to himself as he walked out.

"Yeah. He does." She shrugged.

Brian and Peter were expanding the cat door. The banging and sawing were getting on her nerves and bothering the cats.

Keep cool, Kit.

"Hey guys," she said, raising her voice over the sawing. "Do you think you could do this at night?"

Removing the cat door from the box, Brian gathered the screws. "Sorry, Kit, it's almost done. No more sawing or banging." He winked.

Peter just glared.

CHAPTER 34

Daisy stood by the cat collectibles shop. "Hey, I need you all here!"

Mr. Nuggy walked over, bowed his head, and smiled.

A woman, ignoring the congregating cats, walked around them to head toward the café.

Vee slid around the corner, slammed into the wall, stood up, shook her head, and sat on all fours.

"Why are you calling a meeting? That's my job!" Gabby pushed herself between Vee and Mr. Nuggy.

"When did it become your job?" Vee asked.

"It's always been my job. If you would pay attention instead of chasing feathers, you would know this."

Daisy waved a black cat to come over, only to watch him flicker his tail as he walked into the PP Parlor.

"There is a murderer terrorizing this place, and you're calling a meeting? What if he sees this and targets us next?" Gabby said.

"You called a meeting the other day. What's the difference?" Daisy said.

"Terrorizing? You don't look like a scared cat," Vee said.

"Gabby, no one is going to kill you. You'd talk them to death instead." Daisy grinned at Gabby.

"Fear is an illusion," Mr. Nuggy said.

Gabby looked him up and down and squinted her eyes. "No, it's not. I'm afraid this meeting will bore me to death," Gabby said.

"Where's Trunk?" Daisy asked.

"You still haven't answered my question. Why are you calling a meeting?" Gabby asked.

Daisy sighed. "Gabby, shush."

"Did you just shush me? Why does everybody shush me?"

Vee giggled.

Mr. Nuggy smiled.

"Yes, I did. I'll wait for Trunk. Then I'll begin." Daisy turned her head away from Gabby.

Trunk peeked his head through the cat door in the PP Parlor. "I'll be right there."

"So this is so important that you're going to interrupt a cat doing his business?" Gabby said, sitting down.

"Did you call over Fluffy, whatever his name is, to join us?" Gabby asked.

Daisy sighed. "It's Fluffy Bottom, and no, he is not interested in anything we do."

"Not smart enough, that's why." She sniffed the air. "What is that smell?" Gabby asked.

"Trunk. It can be strong," Vee said.

Gabby looked at Vee. "No, something smells yummy."

"Oh, it's the cookies Craig makes. Smells awesome, huh?" Daisy closed her eyes and sniffed. "Maybe we can get some when we're done. I know that clerk at the cash register. She has given me a few cookies before."

"She has never given me one. I've been here longer than all of you," Gabby said.

"When you meow, everyone looks over. How can she sneak you anything when you always want attention?"

"I'll just steal a cookie," Gabby said.

"You can't. They're in thick bags. Besides, everyone knows where you live."

"I can get into it." Gabby shows everyone her claws. "I have sharp teeth and claws."

"Look at that tiny paw." Vee smiled.

Gabby eyeballed Vee as she tucked her paw under her chest.

"You have a sharp tongue that needs a dull edge," Mr. Nuggy said.

Gabby looked over at Mr. Nuggy. "What? Again, you make no sense."

Trunk walked between the cats and flopped over on his side, landing on Gabby's paw.

"Will you get your butt off of me," she said, pulling her paw from under him.

"I'm glad you are all here." Daisy's green eyes sparkled with delight.

"I wanted to show you my new collar. It's so pretty." Daisy lifted up her chin. A tiny green and gold rhinestone collar glistened in the light.

"That's pretty, Daisy. Where did you get it?" Vee asked.

"You know that family I play with who have the two small girls. They bought it for me."

"The girl who has strawberry milk and spills it on the floor?" Trunk asked.

"Yeah, she spilled it because you stuck your paw in her cup," Daisy said.

"Yummy," Trunk said as he was pushed from behind.

"Get off me!" Gabby shouted as she pushed him with her front paws. "You had a green collar. Why get a new one?" Gabby pushed harder.

"My old collar was dull. I needed more sparkle." Daisy shook her head to adjust her collar.

Trunk shifted his weight, and Gabby removed her foot, falling over.

"Are you having issues, Gabby?" Vee asked.

Squinting her eyes at Vee, she focused on Daisy. "You called us over to tell us about a collar?"

"Yes, I wanted to show you. It's pretty, huh?" Daisy said, smiling.

"It's the color of vomit," Gabby said.

"No, it's not. It's jade. You're just jealous."

"No, I'm not. I don't care about that stuff. My pink collar is perfect for me. No fluff."

"Pink is for sweet girls, Gabby. You are sassy. You should bedazzle that collar with some rhinestones and, for you, spikes." Daisy smiled.

Gabby put her head on her paws.

Daisy looked over at Mr. Nuggy. "Mr. Nuggy has a blue collar. It matches his eyes."

Mr. Nuggy smiled. "Material things don't bring me Zen."

"What about you, Trunk? You like your collar?" Daisy asked.

Trunk looked up from sniffing the floor. "What?"

"Your collar, do you like it?"

"Do I have one?"

Daisy giggled. "Yes, you have a brown collar."

"Oh, good." Trunk continued his sniffing.

"I want a new collar; I've had this one for years." Vee lifted up her chin.

"It's pretty, Vee. I love that red on you. It brings out the yellow hue in your eyes and makes your markings more vibrant."

"Yeah, I guess it is pretty." Vee stood up to allow her collar to settle lower on her neck. A small clump of fur went flying and landed on Gabby's head.Trunk rolled over on his back, feet up in the air. "Look, Gabby has a hat!"

Gabby shook her head, and the piece of fur flew down to her nose. She sneezed, and it landed on her paw.

"Vee, you really need a brush, not a collar," Gabby said, shaking her paw.

"Sorry, Gabby. I got thick fur."

Gabby licked her paw to remove the fur. Now it hung out of the corner of her mouth. She tried to spit it out and talk at the same time.

"Fur got your tongue, Gabby?" Daisy said.

Gabby stopped moving and side-looked at Daisy, a piece of fur still sticking out of her mouth. "I should bite you. I've had it with this dumb collar talk. I want a cookie."

Daisy sighed. "Fine. We have to go to Cat Collectibles and look cute. No yelling, Gabby. Just stand there with your mouth full of fur and sad eyes. Can you do that?"

"Like this?" Gabby opened her eyes wide and wrinkled her forehead.

"Yes! Purrfect."

Trunk squinted his eyes. Daisy giggled and winked at him. "Keep working on it."

They all walked into Cat Collectibles. Daisy gave a soft meow as the cashier looked down. Trunk walked in and stood in the back, squinting his eyes tight.

The cashier looked at Trunk, concerned. "What's wrong, big fella? You look like you're in pain."

Mr. Nuggy walked in front of Trunk and batted his blue eyes.

"Oh, you want cookies?"

Daisy and Vee cooed. Trunk squinted his eyes again. Mr. Nuggy stood on his hind legs. Gabby started to meow, the fur still in her mouth. Daisy looked over, eyeing Gabby.

The cashier removed the fur from Gabby's mouth. "That's better. You are all adorable."

She looked out the glass window toward the Feline Foyer. She saw Sarah, Kit, and the detective talking by the office. No one else was near. She quickly grabbed five cookies from behind the desk. She put one down for each cat.

They all enjoyed their cookies with purrs and pets to follow.

"So spoiled. And I got the best job getting to spoil you," the cashier said with a big smile on her face.

CHAPTER 35

"Kit, can you come in here?" Sarah was shaking her hands.

She stood in front of a large double safe. It had slots and locks on both the left and right sides.

"Do we use this?" Kit asked, wondering why she hadn't noticed it before.

"I've put money into the right slot several times. It always had crap piled up in front of it. Never used the left side. Marjorie was very specific about what side to use. She even made me repeat it before I dropped it in the safe."

Sarah had both sides open. "Look here." She pointed to the left side.

Kit peered in. At the bottom of the safe was a green money bag.

Kit jerked back, her eyes bulging and mouth open. "Is that the bag that was missing?"

"Looks like it. I just thought to check the other side, now that I have a key."

"I'm glad you did. This changes things." Kit twirled her hair. "Let me call Kale back."

"You didn't touch it, right?" Kit asked Sarah as she texted the detective.

Moments later, he appeared at the door. "Are you calling me back to pay for the coffee? I didn't even get to my car."

Sarah pointed to the inside of the safe.

"You found it. Good." He sipped his coffee.

"No, you don't understand. We never use that side of the safe, only the right side," Sarah said.

"So the money bag shouldn't be in the safe?" he asked.

"Yes, but on the right side of the safe, not the left. Sarah has been here seven years and never used the left side."

"Who has access to this office?" he asked, taking his pen and paper out of his pocket.

Kit pointed outside the door at all the people. "If we don't lock it, everyone."

The detective put his gloves on, snapping them. "Whose keys are in the safe?"

"They were Marjorie's. I just gave them to Sarah," Kit said.

He pulled the bag out of the safe, opened it, and saw the money there. "The bag should be locked, right?"

"It should be," Sarah said.

"I'm gonna take this in for printing." He snapped open a bag he had in his pocket.

"There should be five grand in there. Can you let me see it? I can tell if it's all there."

The detective opened the bag. "Just look, don't touch."

Sarah peeked into the bag and checked the money was in individual wraps. "Yup, all there."

"How is Craig?" Kit asked.

The detective leaned against the wall.

"He denied the murder, but was in the break room a half hour before she died. He admitted to stealing the cat food. Who would steal cat food? I don't get it. Just go down to the damn store and grab a bag."

Kit and Sarah both laughed. "That cat food is a specialty blend. A chef makes it. You can't buy it in a store. It's expensive."

The detective shook his head. "I'm in the wrong profession."

He sipped his coffee. He told them about Craig's boss. "When you asked for another batch, he told his boss about borrowing the cat food. Late, but at least he admitted it. The kicker? His boss is his uncle on his mother's side. It's her younger brother, so he can't fire him. She would kill him."

Sarah and Kit looked at each other.

"Did he remember if the money was in the room when he was in there?"

"Marjorie was going through the cash register. He didn't mention the bag. He saw all the money in front of her, yet she refused to pay him his dues. That's when he got mad and left. He was going to see if he could sell his cookies at another cat café until you asked for more."

"I still don't think he did it," Sarah said.

"We have another video to look at today. Might clear him."

The detective walked out of the office, but stopped at Marjorie's memorial table. "Nice set up here."

"Nan's idea, not mine," Kit said.

"It's more than what she deserves," Sarah added.

The detective looked over at Sarah. "You really didn't like her, huh?"

"Nope. She was condescending, overbearing, and mean. I've been doing the work of a manager for years because she was also lazy, but I never got paid. You would be upset too. No, I didn't murder her. I hate the smell of blood. It makes me nauseous." She wrinkled her nose.

Kit put her hand on Sarah. "There has been so much change here recently. Nan left, me coming in, Marjorie dying. Sarah has been a pillar of strength." Sarah grinned at Kit.

"Speaking of Marjorie dying, I gotta get this processed." He held up the plastic bag. "I also need a refill."

"I assume you're going to keep my money for a while?"

"You assume right, Kitty, I mean Kit," he said.

"You're learning."

He handed the bag to another officer and turned back toward the café again.

"You're paying for this cup," Kit said.

He waved again.

Sarah smiled at Kit.

"What? Don't do that. I am not interested right now."

"So you say."

The rest of Thursday was a quiet day. There were a few people who visited Marjorie's memorial table, but most were there for the food. Janice, Peter, and Leanne were the ones who seemed most upset. Leanne surprised Kit. Made her feel she could do better in her own life. Here was a girl who got bullied and embarrassed, and she still cared for Marjorie. She made Kit want to be a better person. Well, at that moment, anyway.

Janice even brought a picture of Marjorie from years ago. Her hair was long and blonde; her beady eyes were brighter. She looked happy in a pink dress. Kit couldn't believe this was the same nasty woman she'd met.

CHAPTER 36

C hecking her watch, Kit leaned over, stretching her legs as she got ready to run. Tilting her head, she put her earbuds in.

The money situation had thrown her off. *Why kill Marjorie? Why leave all that money behind if it was a theft? If you wanted her dead, there had to be a better way. Did Craig do it? Did we blame him for a murder he didn't do?*

That thought made Kit sick to her stomach.

She ran. Her feet hit the pavement hard. She thought about California, running down the West Coast. So much easier there, or was it? Had she forgotten how hard her life was before her job loss? Looking out at this ocean, she focused on the warmth of the sun on her face. The sound of the background music just loud enough to still hear the seagulls and the ocean waves relaxed her instantly.

Sweat dripped down her back as she brought her attention to the music and her conversation with Brenda.

Yes or no answers, huh? That is so dumb.

She heard footsteps behind her. Moving to the right, she expected to see someone sprint by. The booming was getting closer.

She reached over to turn off the music. *Yup, those are footsteps*, she thought.

The footsteps got closer. She turned around fast.

Peter was suddenly running alongside her.

She felt her heart drop to her stomach.

She pulled an earbud out and picked up speed. "Why are you here?" she asked between breaths.

His pace equaled hers.

She pushed harder. He ran faster.

She felt her eyes narrow. *What is going on?* she thought.

"Why are you pushing this investigation? You're not a cop," he said with little breath left.

She ran as fast as she could, leaving him out of breath in the middle of the path.

"You really don't want the murderer found, do you?" he shouted as best he could.

Kit slowed down. She stopped, turned, and walked back to him.

"Of course I do! Why would you think that?" She tried to catch her breath.

"You seem to have a problem with me, Peter. I've done nothing to deserve this," she said between gasps.

"You've picked on Marjorie. Now you're picking on Brian!"

"Brian? What are you talking about?"

"They arrested him today," Peter said.

"Arrested? Brian?" Kit's head spun.

"I hope you're proud of yourself. Stop trying to be a detective. You're hurting people."

He took off running again. Kit sped to catch up with him. Just as she was ready to shout at him, he stopped short and turned. Kit slammed into him, her bad hand folding back awkwardly as it hit his chest.

Flustered, she held her hand and screamed. "Why did you stop?"

Leaning his hands on his knees, he squeaked out, "I'm out of breath."

"Damn it, Peter!" Kit shook her right hand, the pain shooting through her fingers.

She noticed his smirk. He almost looked delighted.

"You think this is funny?" she asked.

Standing up with his hands on his hips. "No. None of this is funny. Many people are getting hurt." He glared at Kit.

"Are you threatening me?" she asked.

He said nothing.

That feeling she'd had the other day when he shot daggers at her with his eyes was back. But instead of getting upset, she got mad. A scene filled her mind...

She kicked him hard in the stomach and watched him fall to the ground. It felt good and got rid of the pain in her hand, even for a moment.

She blinked and saw him clearly again.

"Okay."

Kit turned and sprinted away as fast as she could. The one-word answer she gave him was not as fun as a kick to the stomach. She ran faster, feeling the burn in her lungs.

What an ass, she thought, still shaking the ache out of her hand. Fear crept up her back.

What the hell was going on with Brian?

CHAPTER 37

K it dropped her keys on the dining room table, poured a glass of water, and yanked her phone out to call Detective Flowers.

"Is something going on with Brian?" she shouted.

"Ouch, my ear."

"What is going on? I just returned from my jog. Peter showed up on my run to tell me you arrested Brian," Kit rambled on as she twirled her hair.

"Slow down, Kit. We did not arrest Brian. We're asking him some questions, that's all."

"But why? You spoke to him the other day. What about Craig?" she asked.

Detective Flowers was silent for a moment.

"We checked a video from a house doorbell camera located across the street. We caught his van leaving at the time he mentioned. He's cleared. As for Brian, the fingerprints on the bag are a match."

She dropped into the chair at the table.

"I don't understand what's going on. He didn't steal the money. I don't get it."

"He has a record of stealing from a few years back—one reason he is being questioned. We spoke with Craig. He now remembers the money bag on the table when he was talking to her.

"That's convenient," she said.

"One more thing. There was blood on the money bag."

"I-I..." Unable to get words out, she drew a breath in. "What did he say?"

"He said he found the bag on the floor outside the office. He called her name. She didn't answer. Figured she went home, so he picked it up and put it in the safe. He said he had never used the safe before, so he just put it in the left slot."

Her mind spun. "That makes sense, right? Why murder her, then put the money in the safe? A safe that is locked that he doesn't have access to. What about the cat toy, the sock? Was there blood on that?"

She could feel a tear trickle down her face.

"Damn it, Kale. Answer me!"

"Kit. Give me a bit more time, and I'll come by. We can talk then."

"Fine," she said through gritted teeth.

"I need to search the Pissy, um, back room where he works. Will you give me permission, or do I need to get a search warrant?"

"It's the PP Parlor." For a moment, she couldn't decide what to do. Nan would have been so much better at this. She always kept calm when cat shit hit the fan.

"Kit?"

"Yes."

"Alright, I'll be there soon. Please keep staff out of that room until we get there."

"I can't keep the cats from going in there," she said.

"That's fine. Bye."

Everything around her faded. She leaned over and put her head on her legs until the sensation passed. She sat back up but felt unable to move.

How did I get this wrong? Brian? Craig? Maybe Peter was right. I should have stayed out of it.

Her phone beeped and beeped, but she ignored it. Moving to the couch in a daze, she wrapped herself in a blanket, tucked her knees to her chest, and sobbed.

CHAPTER 38

K it fell asleep on the couch. So much for getting to work on time. Her mind searched for answers, going around and around the clues. She wanted to let it go, needed to let go of this, but she couldn't. That morning would be simple jeans and sneakers. *No dressing up today.* Maybe she'd introduce a dress-down Friday.

She had three phone messages from Sarah and two from Detective Flowers.

Ringing Sarah, she was met with a barrage of questions.

"Yes, Sarah, I heard. I'll be out in a few." She hung up and headed out to the café.

Kit got coffee and a muffin but was stopped by four employees along the way. Everyone was asking about Brian. Everyone was upset. Who could blame them?

Sarah met her at the door, pulling it open before Kit could punch in the code to enter the Feline Foyer.

"Should we postpone that surprise with everything going?" Sarah asked.

"No. It's important. Besides, her mom took a day off work."

"Oh, I forgot," Sarah said. She followed Kit to the office and rambled on about Craig, the murder, and the money bag. At one point, Kit heard nothing. It was all becoming too much. Hoping to avoid the murder talk, Kit shifted topics.

"Did you talk to her mom?"

"Yes, she'll be here in a few, and she's excited. She'll drop her off in front of the café to get a cup of coffee, and then she'll meet her over here."

"Great. See you in a few." Kit walked over to lock the door to the PP Parlor, remembering what the detective had said.

Turning around, she was struck. *This place is beautiful.*

People were in Kitty Cat Collectibles. A staff member placed lights around the shop. The cashier came out and hugged Kit.

You would have never known it had been destroyed last week.

She walked past a few cats on a perch, gave them each a head smooch, and sniffed their fur. That usually made her feel better. This morning she wanted to cry. She walked around the Feline Foyer, talking to staff, giving hugs to those who needed it, and being an ear. She heard little, but her eyes expressed concern.

She then went to the café to do the same. Looking out the window, the ocean was soothing. She continued into the kitchen and gave Janice half a hug. The dishwasher was on the phone, and she immediately put it away as soon as she saw Kit. Being too tired to argue, she let it go and walked through to the Feline Foyer again.

Heading back to the office, Sarah came running up to her. Kit's shoulders sank. "Yes, I know."

Sarah blocked her from the office. "You knew he was a person of interest?"

"I know he's being questioned. I found out this morning. Kale, Detective Flowers, needs permission to search the back room."

"And you didn't call me? You didn't give him permission, did you?" She dropped her arms, her eyes welling up.

Kit held her hands up. "I found out from Peter. He confronted me on the running path this morning. I then called the detective. And yes, I gave him permission. I had to."

Sarah said nothing. She turned toward the bathroom.

Kit stood there watching, then noticed Gabby heading her way.

"Great, more drama," she said out loud.

A cat handler looked at her and looked around.

"That cat is mad at me," she said with a straight face. He gave her a thumbs-up and walked on by.

Kit retreated to the office, where Sarah joined her a moment later, tissue in hand. She hit the couch with a thud. Gabby jumped up, nudged her, and curled up on her lap.

"Sorry about Brian, but he's mine," Gabby said. She meowed at Sarah and began purring.

Kit snorted.

"What's so funny?" Sarah said, anger in her voice.

"The cat."

"What about the cat?"

Sorting paperwork on a tray, Kit sighed. "Never mind, nothing's funny. Do you want to go home? I can handle our guest."

Sarah's eyes were red, and her neck blushed. "I want to hear what the detective said about Brian. I really want... need to talk to Brian." She sniffed. "Did you know he has no family?"

"No, I didn't know that."

"We're his family," she said in an angry tone.

"Sarah, why are you mad at me?"

"It feels like you don't give a shit."

Kit slammed the pile of paperwork down. "What! That is unfair. I have—"

A soft knock on the door stopped the conversation.

"Hey," Detective Flowers said, eyeing both of them. He had on a full suit and tie, looking professional and intimidating at the same time.

"Can you unlock the back room door, please?"

"Nice to see you too," Kit said.

"Just doing my job."

Sarah sat forward. "Detective, can I talk to Brian? He doesn't have any family. He must be really upset."

"Not now. We're still talking to him."

Pulling Gabby in closer, Sarah's voice cracked. "Please."

"Not now," he said, taking the keys from Kit.

Sarah bowed her head into Gabby's chest and cried.

Kit looked at him hard.

"Jesus, you too," he said.

"You're being an ass."

He shrugged and walked out of the office.

Kit ran around the desk, catching him right outside her office. "When you're done, I want you out of my café."

He said nothing as she let the door slam in his face.

Through the window, she watched him meet two other officers. Moving to the other window, she could see them go to the PP Parlor and enter. All the patrons were straining their necks to see what was going on.

Trunk ran out of his newly enlarged PP Parlor door as fast as possible, stopping short by the wall.

She could hear him repeating, "Sit. Sit. Sit." from a distance.

Vee sat in front of the officer guarding the door in the foyer, saying, "Rub my belly." It would almost look inappropriate if she wasn't a cat. The officer glanced down at her, then looked away.

"I need to go to my appointment. Make sure he leaves after they're done."

Sarah said nothing. Gabby nuzzled her, then looked at Kit.

"You took my sock, now my Brian," Gabby said.

Kit felt defeated. "I'll be back in time for our guest."

Sarah nodded. "The card is in the drawer."

CHAPTER 39

K it went back to her apartment to take a breath. A half-hour later, she sat in the waiting room in Brenda's office. The last thing she needed right now was another call from lawyer Ivy. At least here, she was supposed to turn her phone off. Having that break felt good.

Kit shut down around people. The ability to handle different emotions was her sister's thing, being a psychic and all. Instead, Kit would head off to hang with the cats. She didn't have to feel like she had to hold on to their emotions. This was one reason she had a hard time at the warehouse job, being surrounded by men. They complained more than women and expected her to be their ear. All. The. Time.

Brenda's voice broke into her thoughts. "Kit, you can come in now."

The carpet in Brenda's office had changed, switched from brown to a peaceful green with light swirls.

"You changed the area rug."

"You noticed," Brenda said, adjusting herself in her chair and picking up her pen and pad.

Brenda's perfume had a light floral scent. It was relaxing and smelled familiar.

Brenda jumped right in. "So we have a lot to discuss."

"Yup."

"How have these past few days been for you?"

"Like shit."

"Describe shit."

"They questioned the delivery guy. All the clues are adding up. Now my head cat handler has been called in for questioning. They're searching through the back room right now."

"What do you mean, all the clues?"

Kit caught her up on all the information and clues she knew regarding Craig and Brian. She explained how upset her staff and the cats were, especially Gabby.

Brenda flipped through her notebook. "Who is Gabby?"

"The tiny cat who runs the café."

"She's mad at you? How do you know?" Brenda asked.

Kit wondered if she should share her gift. Deciding today was not the day, she continued.

"She's been acting up over the past few days. Hissing at me, biting me."

"So you assume she is mad at you?"

Kit smiled. "You think she's upset by the increase of cops and investigators there?"

"That's a possibility. Have you considered that?"

Kit shrugged.

"How's your anger?"

"I lashed out on the bike path again."

"A bike path, huh? You should stay away from bike paths." She grinned.

Kit put her hands up. "I didn't push anyone, but I did give him hell."

"Who?"

"Peter. He's one of the cat handlers who was good friends with Marjorie. I was running on the path, and he jogged up to me and yelled. He told me about Brian—that they'd pulled him in for questioning. Peter blamed me for it. I was pissed, so I ran after him. He stopped short in the middle of the bike path, and we slammed into each other, squishing my hand. It hurt like hell."

"Did he threaten you?"

Kit looked down. "It felt that way. He made me feel uncomfortable but said nothing threatening. Just blame. He works with Brian, so I can understand why he's upset."

"Brian, the lead cat handler, is under suspicion of murder?"

"The money bag had his prints on it."

"I'm confused."

Kit explained the money bag and prints again as Brenda nodded.

"It sounds like you're involved in this investigation."

"No. I mean, I guess. I seem to find things that help, so I talk it out with the detective and with Sarah. It just happened naturally." Kit leaned forward, shaking her head. "I wish I'd never asked questions. I feel as though I put my employees under the bus. My idea was to move here, work at a tiny cat café, pet a cat, have coffee, and go home."

"It sounds like you're trying to control it all."

"Well, yeah. I am the boss."

Brenda leaned back and softened her voice. "Kit, there is no such thing as control. The only thing we can control is our reaction to life events."

Looking out the window, Kit got caught up watching a bird on a branch. "I liked it better when you gave yes or no answers."

"Speaking of the yes and no, did you try it this week?"

"I did once with Peter. I said, 'Okay,' then ran away. It wasn't intentional. I wanted to get away from him."

"Do you want to try it this coming week?"

"No."

"You did just now. Congratulations."

Kit suppressed a smile. "It's hard to give yes-no answers to a detective who is asking for information *and* to my staff who want more answers."

"Understandable," Brenda said. She took a sip of water. "Your life is messy right now, so I don't want to get into it too much. I want you to continue with trying the yes and no answers. I also want you to journal."

Kit looked at her. "Journal? Are you kidding me?"

Brenda softened her voice again. "Hear me out. I don't want you to write a book, although your story would be a good one. Instead, grab a piece of paper, and every time you get mad, number your anger from one to ten. One being very mild and ten being blood-red mad. Next to that, jot down your reaction."

"My reaction?" Kit asked.

"What you did. Yelled, punched something, went ballistic, suppressed it."

"I have a visualization technique I use when I get pissed," Kit said.

"Oh, that's good. What do you visualize?"

Kit laughed. "I often visualize killing people."

Brenda looked up. "Okay."

"One-word answers again."

"I'm thinking. Not what I expected. Most visualization techniques are visualizing a relaxing place, color therapy," Brenda said. "I have to ask. Do you feel homicidal?"

Kit thinks. "Not really. I just want to get rid of my anger, and these visions pop up. Afterward, I feel better."

"Write them down."

Kit looked at her sideways. "They're pretty gross."

"I can handle gross, provided these are visualizations and not plans you're going to carry out." She pointed her pen at Kit.

"I'm being honest, really."

"Alright."

"Is that it?" Kit asked.

"No. You mentioned you don't like dealing with every-one's emotions. However, your anger is an emotion, and those around you must deal with it. They had to deal with Marjorie when she got angry—"

"I am not Marjorie!"

"No, you're not." Brenda paused. "Marjorie pressed your buttons, right?"

"She never pressed buttons. She would rip them out with her teeth," Kit said.

Brenda put her pen down. "Can you agree that some of your outbursts are similar?"

Kit squeezed the arm of the chair tight. The veins in her neck stuck out. *She picked up a lamp and flung it across the room at Brenda. Her stupid pen went flying. Wonder what one word she has for that.*

Brenda leaned forward with concern.

"Where were you?"

"I had my homicidal moment," Kit said.

"You visualized hurting me?" Brenda asked, leaning back.

"Visualizing is more like it, right? I am not Marjorie," Kit said through gritted teeth.

"First off, I am glad you shared your visualization. I was giving you something to observe, not stating she was anything like you. What I want you to remember is sometimes we can see clearly what others do but not recognize that same behavior in ourselves. I am not judging you—"

"Like hell, you're not!" Kit walked out the door.

She heard Brenda call, "Next Tuesday!"

"Why is he still here?" Kit said as she saw Detective Flowers talking to Sarah.

"He let me speak to Brian," Sarah said with a half smile. "He told me the story from years ago. It was a bogus claim about stealing. There were two brothers that owned the company. One liked Brian, the other didn't. The one who didn't like him wanted him gone, so he made a false claim about stealing. Once he left the company, they didn't file the charge. The brother got what he wanted."

Kit looked at the detective. "You're still here?"

He walked past the desk and stood in front of Kit. "Why are you so mad at me? I am doing my job. I am following the clues you left for me. Just because you had a bad day, don't take it out on me."

Biting her lip, Kit said nothing.

"How much longer are you going to keep him?" Sarah asked.

Detective Flowers ignored the question. "What was the argument he had with Marjorie?"

"It was about ordering cat litter. She waited until the last minute to order it. She liked to press his buttons," Sarah said.

Kit thought, *Buttons again.*

"What about Craig?" Kit said.

"He's no longer a suspect."

Looking shocked, Sarah pulled at his arm. "What about the sock? There was blood on it and on his cart, right?"

He was looking down at Sarah's hand, which was still on his jacket. She moved it as he backed up.

"Yes. I mean, no." He shook his head. "There was no blood on the sock. It was red frosting. She put catnip on the floor, so that could have happened when he got there or when he left. He said she opened the catnip first and sprinkled it around. He didn't take the money, and we saw him on the neighbor's camera leaving at the time he said he left. Plus, there was no blood on his shoes or clothes."

"I saw him get in her face at the party," Sarah said.

"Arguments don't always mean murder, Sarah," he said, looking at Kit. "He told her to shove it and that he was going to tell his uncle. She would have nothing to blackmail him with. Marjorie laughed at him. He said he left after that."

Kit had nothing to say. Not even one word, so she walked out of the office.

CHAPTER 40

K it returned to see Sarah laughing with another employee. It seems the detective was gone, and Sarah was in a better mood. Sarah, Kit remembered, was good at hiding her true feelings. But then, it had been years. Things might have changed.

Kit headed for her office, kicked her shoes off, and tossed on slipper socks. Her emotions were raw. Brenda told her she was Marjorie. Those words echoed in her mind.

She stepped back out of the office and almost slammed into Janice. Janice frowned and looked down at her.

"Why do you look shorter?"

Lifting her slippered foot up, Kit smiled.

Janice laughed and pointed at her feet. "Be careful in those. If you step in loose catnip, you'll go flying on your butt. "

"Thanks. Didn't even think of that," Kit said.

Kit went back into her office, forgetting why she'd walked out. Today felt off, and nothing could take the dread out of her mood. Getting cozy in her slipper socks was something she did at her previous job. She was putting her shoes back on as Sarah walked in with a card. The card, that was why she had walked out.

"Here, sign this," she said.

Kit signed it and handed it back to Sarah. "Are you okay?"

"No, but I'll deal with it for now." Sarah leaned her head out the door of the office. "Our guest is here."

"Wonderful," Kit said. She followed Sarah into the Feline Foyer.

"Leanne!" she called, noticing the girl's hair was still white.

"You told my m-mom to bring me in here," Leanne said quietly, eyes wide. "Am I-I in t-t-trouble?"

"Not at all," Sarah said.

Kit looked up to see a woman with brown hair, glasses, and a similar smile standing behind her.

Kit reached out and shook her hand.

"Hello. Thanks for bringing Leanne by."

She smiled and nodded.

"Let's sit over here, okay?" Sarah guided Leanne to the chair in front of the office. Leanne could see Peanut Butter being brought out of the PP Parlor in a cat carrier. He had no collar on.

She jumped up. "Are you-you getting rid of P-p-peanut B-b-utter?"

"Yes, but it's good. He's going home with you," Sarah said. The cat handler put him next to her.

"Me-e? Mom?" She looked at her mom, then at Sarah, and up at Kit.

Her mom nodded. "Yes, Leanne. I talked to Kit the other day. Peanut Butter is your cat now." She smiled.

Leanne started crying. "P-p-peanut B-b-butter, we are going h-home!"

She frowned for a moment and looked up at Kit. "Do I-I have to bring him... b-b-back?"

Kit giggled. "No, he's going to be your cat. You take care of him, and you keep us updated."

Sarah handed her the card, and they watched her read it as more tears flowed.

Sarah whispered in Kit's ear. "Get ready for the hug. A big one is coming."

And just like that, Leanne was on her feet, slamming her body into Kit, almost knocking her to the ground.

Kit said in a muffled voice. "Sarah suggested the gift card." She was on Sarah with a bear hug just as fast.

Kit tapped Leanne on the shoulder. She let go of Sarah. "Leanne, that gift is from all of us. You can get a few toys for Peanut Butter. Plus, he needs a new collar. Peter will bring you a cat litter box, litter, a bowl, and some food. You can see him on the way out. There is one thing. Brian is going to need help cleaning the cat litter boxes. Would you be interested in volunteering for a few months?"

Her eyes lit up. "Y-y-yes." She looked down. "I wish B-b-Brian was here."

"We do too. He'll be back soon, and we'll tell him how happy you are and that you'll be working with him." Kit felt a sting of guilt telling her something that may not be true.

Leanne approached to hug Kit again, but she spun her toward the Kitty Cat Collectibles. She smiled and bounced over to the shop, her white hair bouncing with her.

Her mom stood with Kit and Sarah. "Thank you so much. She loves it here, and she loves that cat so much." She looked down at Peanut Butter.

Kit looked at Leanne's mom. "Leanne is a nice girl, and she treats Peanut Butter so well." She leaned down to peer into the carrier. "You'll be in expert hands, buddy." The cat meowed.

As her mom walked toward the gift shop, Sarah noticed Peter struggling to get the supplies for Leanne out of the PP Parlor's door. She sighed. "I hope Brian comes back. I can't imagine Peter taking over. He can't even carry a cat's litter tray and litter at the same time. He's going to drop it everywhere."

She winced as the cat tray hit the floor. "Good grief," Sarah said.

"Hey, I have an appointment in a few hours. Gonna head out," Kit said.

"Alright. I need to help Peter out before the bag of litter hits the floor too." Sarah winced again as she walked toward Peter, who was still trying to balance everything in his arms.

"I agree," Kit looked toward the big window. The cats congregating. *Something is happening*, she mused.

CHAPTER 41

Vee padded over to Gabby, who was sunning herself on a bench in front of the window.

"Where is Peanut Butter going?" Vee said. Her green eyes glimmered in the window's light.

Gabby lifted her head. "He's going with that chick over there. The white-haired one. The hugger."

"Peanut Butter loves her!" Daisy said as she joined the conversation. Vee was distracted by Daisy's' tail and began pawing at it.

Rolling her eyes, Daisy took a step back. "I'm not a feather, Vee."

Vee stopped and sat down. "I hope they don't start sending us out of here."

"Nah, they won't. They need us. They can't have a cat café without cats. Peanut Butter was too shy for this place. He only came out for pink, blue, white, or whatever color hair she had. I change the litter less often than she changes hair," Gabby said, now sitting up with her paws folded under her chest.

"You don't change the litter box. Brian does," Daisy said.

Gabby squinted at her. "You know what I mean."

"Speaking of litter, I need to talk to Brian. There are way too many cats using my litter box," Daisy said.

"No one has their own box, Daisy. We all share."

"Well, I think those of us with seniority should get our own boxes." She stood up, plumping her chest.

Gabby rolled her eyes as she watched Mr. Nuggy pad slowly toward Peanut Butter's cat carrier. He stuck his nose in the front grate, blinked, and meowed. Peanut Butter meowed back.

Mr. Nuggy meandered to Gabby.

"What did you say to him?" Vee asked, but her eyes were on his tail, up in the air, moving back and forth.

He paused, blinked slowly a few times. "I said, 'Meow.'"

Gabby stared at him. "Meow? What the hell is that? That is your departing wisdom from a Zen cat?"

Mr. Nuggy stood still and simply looked at them. His blue eyes were pale from the light of the window. Vee eyed his tail again while Gabby and Daisy sat back down.

"Have any of you heard him talk?" He looked around to see blank stares. "Have any of you ever talked to him?" he asked. Again, blank stares.

"Just as I thought. Peanut Butter does not talk. He is a cat who meows. Therefore, my wisdom is a 'meow.'"

Gabby turned her head to look away.

"Now I go eat," he said and turned his back on the group.

"Wait, I have something to talk about," Gabby said, almost shouting.

He looked back at her. "Let me guess, your sock?"

"Yes, my sock."

All the cats grumbled as they walked away.

Mr. Nuggy stopped, looked back at Gabby. "You lost your sock, you had your sock, and you lost your sock again. Am I right?"

Gabby stood alone. "Yeah, but why? I don't know if I really miss my sock," she said in a raised voice.

"Your sock wasn't what you were missing, Gabby." Mr. Nuggy turned away.

"I wish you would talk like a normal cat like you did last year. I understand a 'meow' better than that stupid wisdom." She plopped down, ready to close her eyes to think about her dilemma, when a string held by a child passed by her nose. Ignoring it, she drifted away.

CHAPTER 42

K it snuck back into her apartment after Leanne got Peanut Butter. She slept hard for what felt like days. It was morning. She rolled to face the ocean, looking through puffy eyes. She wanted to cry more, but there was nothing left. It was too much. The move. The murder. Her friends being mad at her. Craig. Brian. Even Gabby was mad at her. Not to mention the comment that Brenda made hurt like hell. Everyone was against her. Today, even the beauty of the ocean couldn't seem to wash away the sorrow of the day, at least not yet.

"I should have never moved," she said out loud.

She reached for her cell phone.

A text read, *I left something for you at the front door.*

"I hope it's coffee." Her feet hit the floor.

She peeked out her apartment door. Nothing. *Must be the office door. Rats!*

She padded back in and threw on a hoodie, sweatpants, and slippers. She looked at her clock. At least no one would be in the café yet.

Keys in pocket, she took her phone and snuck down the hallway, looking around for anyone, just in case. She'd gotten right near her office when she ran into Janice, who was exiting the kitchen.

Her hand slammed into Janice, sending the phone flying.

"Shit!" She grabbed her hand but still tried to get her phone. Janice reached down at the same time, and they bumped heads.

"Ouch," they both said.

Janice readjusted her glasses. "Kit, oh no...I'm sorry. I thought no one was here." Janice rubbed her head.

Kit bit her tongue and held her hand, then rubbed her head. "You have a hard head."

"Been told that." Janice put her hand out to stop Kit from moving. She leaned over and picked up Kit's phone. "You didn't break your screen, but you dented the side," she said, wiping it off.

You need a protector." She pulled out her own phone to show Kit.

"We have the same phone, and this thing can tolerate a lot of drops."

"What happened to your phone?" The case was dented in one corner.

"Oh. Yeah. I dropped it," she said, shoving it back in her pocket as she handed Kit her phone.

"Are you going to be okay, Kit?"

"Yup." *One-word answer*, she thought.

"I can get you some ice for your hand and head," Janice said, cracking a smile.

"No. I gotta grab something and get back in my apartment before the entire staff sees me in my pjs. Janice, do me a favor? Let Sarah know I won't be in today. Unless it's an emergency, I prefer not to be called."

"No probs. Enjoy your day off," she said as she walked back into the kitchen, the door swinging behind her.

Kit noticed Trunk lying on the floor. As she walked by, he said, "Sit. Sit. Sit."

"Damn, you're like a parrot, boy. We need to teach you another word."

He purred.

The package was on the steps. She unlocked the door, grabbed it, and headed to her apartment. She pulled the peas out of the freezer again, made coffee, kicked her slippers off, and opened the package to find Gabby's sock.

Kit's shoulders sank.

"I was looking for chocolate. Darn," she said, pushing the box away.

She woke to the loudest meow she had ever heard. She looked around in a panic as she rubbed the sleep out of her eyes. A quick nap on the couch had turned into a long snooze.

"Meow!"

"Again with the meowing." Kit opened her door, and Gabby stuck her nose in the apartment. She padded in, tail in the air.

"You must have a homing device attached to your tail."

Gabby jumped on the back of the couch. "Why?"

Kit nodded. "See that open box on the dining table? Your sock is in it."

Gabby's eyes went wide. She ran past Kit and hit the table at high speed. Reaching into the box, it tipped over.

"My sock!" She flipped it in the air. She played with it for about a minute, then lay down.

Kit joined her at the table. "That's it? I thought you would be more excited. You've driven me nuts about that darn sock."

Gabby curled her paws under her chest. "When is Brian coming back?" she asked, voice low.

"I dunno."

"I miss him picking me up every morning for my morning squeeze."

"You want a hug?" Kit asked, putting her hands out.

"No. Not the same." Gabby sighed. "He carried me around every night before he left. We would make rounds together. He would lift me up on his shoulder. It was our time."

"You want to hang with me today? Just me and you. I'll let Peter know where you are."

She stretched and put her hand on her sock. "Sure, I have nothing else to do."

"Geez, make me feel worse, will ya?" Kit said as Gabby jumped up on the couch, kneaded the blanket, and curled up near her.

After the second movie, Kit headed to the bathroom, and Gabby followed. She jumped on the bed and gave her head a cleaning.

As Kit walked out of the bathroom, Gabby said, "Mr. Nuggy told me something the other day. "

Kit giggled.

"What's so funny?"

"The name. Mr. Nuggy. Where did it come from? Is it from his nuggets of wisdom, or did they name him after a chicken nugget?"

Gabby cocked her head to one side. "Thanks. I'm hungry now."

"The last time you ate in this apartment, you told me the food and I tasted like cardboard."

"Well, you did!"

Kit went to the kitchen, put crackers and cheese on a plate, and gave Gabby a few cat treats. Both ended up back on the couch. Gabby fell asleep with her feet up in the air. Kit watched her. She was adorable when she wasn't being a sassy cat. Kit realized it had been years since she'd talked to a cat like this. She often thought of her gift as a burden. Tonight it was a gift.

Kit thought about Sarah. No text messages. There was still a murderer loose, and she couldn't shake the comments from the one person who was supposed to be her support. Brenda.

"I am *not* Marjorie," she said out loud, waking up Gabby.

Gabby yawned and stretched her paws out. She jumped down, grabbed her sock, and headed for the door. She meowed.

"Where are you going? Thought we were going to hang out together. Misery loves company?"

"You're the one who's miserable. I don't want that kind of energy in my life," Gabby said.

"You were sulking all day. What changed?"

"I am purrfect the way I am. I don't need to change," she said, puffing out her chest. "Mr. Nuggy told me that. Um, maybe you are purrfect for a human."

"How nice. The cat finds enlightenment." Kit rolled her eyes and headed to the door to open it.

"Thanks for hanging with me. Oh, what else did Mr. Nuggy tell you?"

Gabby dropped her sock. "Something about not having what you want. Or having what you want but not knowing you have it. Or having it now—"

"So now that you have your sock, you don't want it?"

"I'm thinking I'm better without it," Gabby said as she picked up the sock, leaving Kit behind.

"I wish you decided that a week ago."

Kit closed the door. A second later, she was in a heap in front of the door, bawling her eyes out.

"What is wrong with me?" she cried as she put her hands to her face and kicked her feet like a two-year-old.

CHAPTER 43

The afternoon was hard. Kit kept hearing Brenda's words echo in her mind. She sat in her recliner, looking out toward the ocean.

Earlier, they released Craig. He phoned Kit and Janice. He was upset and felt betrayed that no one went to bat for him. Kit explained that she only reported what she found. He apologized for his outburst at the PP Parlor. He said two or three times, "I told you I didn't do it."

Kit felt the knot in her stomach expand.

"How did I get this so wrong? What am I doing getting involved, anyway?" She slammed her fist on the recliner armrest and shouted.

She jumped as her doorbell rang. "Who is it?"

"Sarah!"

"It's open. Come in," Kit said.

Sarah walked straight to Kit's chair. "You told me you had an appointment."

"Yeah." She dropped her head down. "Sorry about that. I really needed a time-out."

"You lied to me."

Kit rocked in the chair. "I guess I did. This has been overwhelming."

"I thought we had trust. I thought we were friends," Sarah said.

"Really. It was a mention of an appointment, that's all. I came back here, where I've been sitting for about an hour. I was afraid I'd panic and start throwing shit, then end up in jail too."

Tears welled up in Sarah's eyes. "Well. You are not the only one who is trying really hard to hold it together." She began sobbing. "Thanks for worrying about your friends, or should I say employees."

She turned and walked out. The door slammed.

"Great! Just great. What else can go wrong?" Kit looked up at the ceiling. "Never mind. Rhetorical question."

Kit leaned the chair back, held the pillow tight, and sniffed.

When she woke up, it was dark. She dragged herself to bed and hid under the covers.

How did this all go so wrong?

CHAPTER 44

"**I**'m coming over."

"No, please. I just need some space."

"Okay, hold on, gurl. My camera is not on. Can you see me now?" Tess said.

"Can you see me?" Kit asked.

Leaning back, Tess made a face. "Dang! You look like shit! What's going on?"

"I'm thinking about going back to California."

"You just got here. We haven't caused trouble yet," Tess said with a smile. "Have you talked to Nan about it?"

"I'm torn." Kit looked away. "I don't want to disappoint her. She thought I could handle this job."

"Kitty, what are you talking about?"

She filled her in on everything that had happened, even the cats.

Tess nodded. "Ah, so you want to run back to the place you just left. The place you hated. You've been gone just long enough to forget how miserable you were." Tess took a sip of soda. "Jeez, gurl. You need to get over yourself. A manager with ten years experience couldn't handle all that."

"But Sarah—"

"Sarah is hurting. Just like you, sweetie. She would have never been that upset over something so small if she wasn't."

"I was told by my counselor that I'm like Marjorie."

Tess took another sip. "What did she say exactly?"

Kit shrugged.

"Kitty Cat, you don't always listen to what people really say. When you get mad, you shut off your ears. I know you're probably doing it now."

"What?" Kit said, smiling.

"Funny."

"Tess, I am always angry. I can't seem to shake it."

"You've always been this way."

"No, I haven't. I was a calm person."

"You might have been calm when you were five. The only reason you didn't lash out is that you became a hermit. You can't lash out at people if they aren't there. Then you took a job in a warehouse. Not the best place to socialize."

"You're not helping, Tess." Kit sank in her chair, twirling her hair.

"Okay. I'm making a point. You're a good person, got a big heart. You don't need to change your personality, just the way you react to things." Tess looked at Kit, who was moving out of view on the video.

"Kit?"

Kit moved back into view. "That's what she meant."

"What? Who?" Tess asked.

"Gabby. She thinks I could be a purrfect human."

"Purrfect? Oh, Gabby." Tess clicked her tongue. "Smart cat. Maybe you should see her instead of the counselor. Kit, you *are* purrfect the way you are. And you sleep like a cat. How long did you stay in bed today?"

"All day."

"It's about time you get over yourself, put your boots on, and kick it. No kicking people. Feeling better, gurl?"

"A little, yeah. I need to call Sarah first."

"Does she know about the cats?"

"No."

"It might give her more perspective on why it's so overwhelming."

"Good point. You still coming over?" Kit said.

"Nah, you're good now. Besides, if you smell the way you look, I want nothing to do with you, gurl."

Kit laughed. "Thanks, Tessy, you da best!"

Kit threw her a kiss and turned off the video.

CHAPTER 45

C leaning the kitchen was never something Kit liked to do. She enjoyed it about as much as cleaning a cat litter pan. But today it needed to get done, and she needed to do something easy. She called Brenda to schedule her appointment, which was supposed to be on Tuesday but was moved to Monday afternoon. *Two sessions in, four hundred to go,* she thought as she wiped the microwave, which she had been cleaning for a while. Using her left hand made the job harder, and not paying attention didn't help.

She tried to use her right hand, to no avail.

"Damn it!"

Taking a breath, she thought about a book Brenda emailed her to read. She tossed the rag in the sink, hit the couch, and looked it up on her e-reader. She adjusted her pillow as the download started. Five minutes later, she threw the reader on the couch. Nope. Reading a book about anger was making her angrier.

"This is not working," she said out loud as she got back up. Instead, she took a shower.

With her hair in a towel, she made the call she'd been dreading. Her heart raced.

"Sarah?"

"Yeah."

"Can you stop by tomorrow morning? Are you there?"

"Yeah, I'm here," Sarah said.

"Can you come by?"

"I got a few errands to run. I'll be by around ten."

"Thank you, I'll—Hello? She hung up on me. Seriously?" Kit ran the towel through her hair.

"And I'm the one with issues. Blame Kit for her unacceptable behavior. Get mad at Kit because she tried to help find a murderer. Get pissed at Kit because of a tiny little lie about a meeting. What the—ah, screw it."

She walked back into the bathroom.

Kit stood by the kitchen, watching Janice cook. When she tapped on the door, Janice jumped.

"Sorry. I didn't mean to startle you. Are you planning on staying long? It's getting late."

"Nah, just waiting for one more thing to get out of the oven."

"Okay, let me know when you leave, so I can lock up. I'll be in the office."

Janice put her thumb up. "Hey, Kit? Any news on the investigation?"

"Nope. As you know, Craig is off the hook. Brian is still a person of interest, but I really don't think he did it. We're talking Brian here, the one person who hates violence of any kind."

Janice moved scones from a tray to another plate. "Yeah, could be anyone. We never lock that back door at night except when we leave."

"Really?

Huh?" Kit looked at the door.

"Oh, Janice?"

Janice jumped a bit. Her eyes went wide.

"Great job you're doing," Kit said with a smile.

Janice dropped her shoulders. "Thanks, Kit."

When Kit got to her office, she left the door ajar. Deep in paperwork, she heard a meow and a soft scratching. A smile crossed her face as a little black paw pushed its way through. Behind her, another cat followed.

"Good evening, Mr. Nuggy."

He bowed his head.

"Sure, don't say hi to me!" Gabby said.

Kit picked up Gabby and kissed her on the head before a paw extended to push her nose.

"Why does everyone kiss me?" she asked.

Kit moved her paw and gave Gabby a hug. She settled in with purrs. "This is work harassment," Gabby said in a soft voice as she leaned in.

"Well, considering I'm HR, you can tell me all your woes," Kit said.

Gabby squirmed free and went next to Mr. Nuggy.

"I told him you had a question," Gabby said.

"I do?

"Yeah, you asked me what he told me about."

"Yes, that's right." *Go with it, Kit*, she thought. "I was wondering—"

There was a rap on the glass. Kit pulled the blinds aside. Janice gave her a thumbs-up.

Kit called, "Lock the door. I'll see you Monday."

Gabby was watching Mr. Nuggy out of the corner of her eye.

"Yes, Gabby?"

"When she's done, I want to tell you something," she said in a high-pitched voice.

"Patience, grasshopper," Mr. Nuggy said as he turned his attention back to Kit.

"Gabby said something to me about being perfect the way I am. How can I be perfect when I have all these flaws? I get mad; I lash out. How can I be perfect this way?"

Gabby leaned forward. "I'm purrfect."

"Yes, Gabby, I know," Kit said.

Mr. Nuggy blinked and shifted his weight. "Gabby is perfect in her own way." He winked. "Humans try hard to be what they are not. But you are only who you are."

Kit shook her head, wondering if getting advice from a cat was a good idea. "I don't understand."

"You are human and have emotions. They are neither right nor wrong. They just are. It's only when we judge them do they feel wrong."

"But my emotions and outbursts are not healthy."

"Emotions are not bad or good. They just are. You can control how you use the emotions you have."

Mr. Nuggy was a beautiful red-pointed Siamese with a cream-colored body and blue eyes that matched his collar where a gold charm dangled. His eyes were so vibrant, it felt like he looked into her soul.

"Gabby's sock went missing. She was angry. Was that okay?" Kit asked.

"Yes. When her sock went missing, it was supposed to be missing. When she found it, it was supposed to be found. She was angry. That was reality. Humans want to change reality. Everything is perfect the way it is because it is the way it is."

Gabby said quietly, "I am so over that sock."

Kit rolled her eyes as Gabby looked at Kit and then at Mr. Nuggy.

"Wait a minute. Why are you explaining all of this to her? When I asked you about my sock, you only gave me one of your stupid lines."

"Would you have listened?" Mr. Nuggy said.

She put her head on her paws with a soft meow.

"Thanks, Mr. Nuggy," Kit said, feeling as though she should bow or something.

Gabby paused, but Mr. Nuggy walked out.

"I needed to tell you something," Gabby said.

"What?"

"I don't remember."

Kit laughed as Gabby stomped her paws in front of her.

"I am going to tell everyone you are getting advice from a cat."

Leaning down, Kit whispered, "Yeah? Well, I'll tell your friends you cuddled with me on the couch. For hours. And you let me rub your belly."

Gabby opened her mouth. "I never let you rub my belly!"

"How do you know? You were sleeping on my couch, snoring," Kit said.

She leaned back. "I don't snore!"

Kit shrugged her shoulders and smiled.

Gabby padded out the door and turned around. Her eyes were big, her mouth still open.

"You wouldn't!" she said, frowning.

Kit winked and closed the door.

CHAPTER 46

B reathing heavily, she felt good on the run. Pausing in the middle of the path, she could see the windy path ahead and the cat café in the distance behind her. It was a remarkable building and on the ocean. Nan had done well.

She watched a man and his dog run at a perfect pace. The dog smiled, his collar clanking in a rhythm. Not to disturb them, she stepped to the edge of the grass. The man waved.

As she stood there, she remembered the times her sister, Sky, would play games out here. They would knock each other off the path and roll down the embankment on the soft sand.

"Pushing people off the path started in my childhood. Huh." She smirked and took off running back to the café.

At the last moment, she headed toward the ocean. She ran at full speed into the ocean. The cold water slammed into her, rattling her senses. She pulled her ponytail out of her hair with her right hand. For the first time in weeks, it felt better. She smiled as the water wrapped around her, calming her nerves as it soothed her soul.

She stood there, eyes closed, the waves rocking her back and forth.

She repeated, "I'm perfect, I'm perfect."

A minute later, her thoughts streamed. *How can I be perfect? Brian is still under suspicion. I was an ass to Detective Flowers. Sarah's still pissed and—*

"Oh, stop, Kit!" she said out loud and slapped the water.

Running from the ocean to the café, she was eager to talk to Sarah but worried about how telling Sarah about her gift would go.

Sarah arrived. Kit felt the tension in the air. She wanted to talk, to make it go away, but then remembered what Mr. Nuggy said about things being the way they were. She poured coffee in silence and went to the patio. Clematis climbed on the brick between her patio and the café's open space. A breeze hit her face, and she remembered being out there earlier.

She cleared her throat.

"Sorry, Sarah. My lie hurt you. I was not thinking about anyone else. I was selfish."

"I thought I was going to pass out when I heard Brian was a person of interest," Sarah said.

Kit gasped. "I didn't know."

Sarah looked ahead. "I thought you were my friend, not just a boss. I needed you."

"You are my friend. And you're right. I should have talked to you. It's...um...sometimes...well, lately, I'm afraid of lashing out, of getting angry. I've found it easier to just leave."

"You did that years ago too." Sarah sipped her coffee. "The last time you were here, you argued with your grandmother. You stormed out. I asked her if I should go get you. She told me no, let you be."

"Hmm. I don't remember that."

"I do," Sarah said.

"Well, I guess I have to adult a bit more."

Sarah smiled. "Yeah. You got some work to do. Listen Kit , I can tolerate your outbursts and your anger. I'll even toss you a cat or drag you out of a difficult situation, but I can't tolerate being lied to."

"I'll try harder," Kit said, holding back tears, hoping that it wasn't another lie.

"Can I ask you an honest question?" Kit asked, tucking her hair behind her ear.

"Sure." Sarah put her feet up in her chair.

"Do you think I'm like Marjorie?"

"What!? No, not at all. Why would you ask me that?"

"She was mean. I can be mean, and I know that I've made people uncomfortable with my outbursts."

Sarah placed her hand on Kit's arm. "You are nothing like her. She was mean and vindictive—a horrible person. Come on. Even you noticed how different the energy is around here now that she's gone."

Kit kept her head down. She ran her fingers around the top of her coffee mug. "I have something else we need to talk about."

"Alright, but I can't right now. I need to meet my mother for brunch. Can I come back later?"

Kit puffed and blew out a breath.

"Yeah." She leaned over and gave Sarah a hug.

As Sarah walked out, Kit listened to Sarah's keys jingle.

"The collar!" She jumped to her feet.

CHAPTER 47

In the afternoon, Sarah arrived with two cups of coffee in her hands and a smile on her face.

"You look happy. What gives?" Kit said.

"I had a nice day with my mom. I needed some perspective."

"How so?" Kit asked as they hit the couch. Sarah dropped her bag by her feet as she sank into the corner of the couch. Kit crossed her legs and sipped the coffee.

"She reminded me I take things personally. I shouldn't have gotten mad at you before."

"No, you had every right. I need to learn to talk to people and not to shut down."

"I am glad we talked, Kit. Thank you."

Kit smiled, wondering what to do next. "Did you bring your laptop?"

"Oh, yeah, right here." Sarah put it on the table and pulled up the cat tracker program. "What are you looking for?" she asked.

"I'm looking for Gabby's collar information. I want to see where she went the night of the murder."

Sarah looked up. "Why?"

"Hold on." Kit turned the computer screen toward Sarah. "Look!"

Kit started scrolling through a few days.

"That's Gabby." Sarah points.

Kit grins. "That's the office."

Sarah looked at it. "I don't get it."

Kit put her hand on Sarah's arm. "We have Brian's alibi. Gabby!"

"I still don't get it." Sarah moved the computer closer, moving the screen around.

"Let me text the detective. Can you copy the file from three days prior to the murder and on the night of the murder from about eight forty to nine? I want to send them to the detective."

"Sure. I hope you'll fill me in," she said, side-eyeing Kit.

Kit texted the detective with her findings. He texted back that he would look at it.

She pulled the computer from Sarah and scrolled back two days prior. She pointed.

"Gabby told me—um—a cat handler told me that Brian carried Gabby when he made his nightly rounds of the café. If he carried her, her tracking chip would show where he went. See, this is Thursday. Same route. Friday, same. Now, here's Saturday. He starts off in the same direction, but then there's a pause, and then they head into the office. He never goes into the break room!"

Sarah's eyes went wide. Her mouth dropped open. "You've cleared Brian!"

"Well, Gabby did. I remembered her collar, the dog running with the collar clanking, and your jingly keys. I remember Nan telling me about the tracker. She wanted the cats to be safe, and she wanted to make the café better for them. Monitor how they travel around it."

Kit heard a beep. She looked at the text and frowned.

She texted, *Yes, it proves he is innocent. How can a cat enter an office door that is closed?*

She watched the three dots move as the detective typed.

Oh. Good point. I'll have my tech guys look at it. If it's accurate, it should clear him.

Kit shook her fist. "Yes! He's gonna have the tech guys look at it. Brian will be cleared!"

She sat back, tipped her head up, and exhaled.

CHAPTER 48

K it sat in Brenda's waiting room, reminiscing about yesterday. Sarah stayed for a few hours. They did a few high fives, danced around, and laughed. It felt good to laugh. For the first time in a few weeks, Kit felt like she could breathe. Yes, there was still a murder left to solve, but Brian was not under investigation, so there was that.

Detective Flowers let Brian go. He said Brian was lucky the tracker was functional. Brian was so excited he stopped by the cat café around seven. He greeted them and the cats, who swarmed all around him.

Gabby got her cuddles and head smooches ad nauseam. The others got nauseated watching. It delighted Gabby that her favorite human was back.

Even Sarah went in for a hug. Kit got half a hug, mostly because Gabby wouldn't get off his shoulder.

Even with all the excitement, reality sank in. There was still a murderer loose. Kit ran it through her mind. Craig was innocent. A neighbor on the street by the café saw his van. A cat tracker proved Brian's movements, and he didn't enter the break room. Janice took the catnip and food, then broke in a few days later. Stupid to go back for evidence, but her prints were only on those two items.

Who else could have committed the murder? Peter? Sarah? Another employee that Kit doesn't know about. Who else hated it there?

Brenda opened the door. "Good morning. You look different today."

Kit smiled. "Did you know I am perfect?"

Brenda eyed Kit. "Really?"

Kit chuckled. "The one-word answers again."

"Tell me about this new perfect you."

Kit told her the story but not who said it.

"Interesting theory," Brenda said, rubbing her chin. "Perfection is an illusion. We all have flaws, issues, and human experiences that color our life. You are a perfect representation of a human, which would make you perfect. But..."

"But what?" Kit could feel her excitement waning as if a cloud just rolled in.

"Human actions have consequences even if you are perfect."

Kit rocked her chair hard. "You know, you told me the other day that I'm just like Marjorie. It weighed on my mind the whole weekend. It made me feel like shit. That I'm no good. Just a nasty, angry person like that bitch. And now, when I come in here in a good mood, finally letting it go, you tell me how imperfect I am. How is this helping me feel better?"

"Let's break that down. I said your actions were like Marjorie's. Actions, Kit, not personality or anything else.

Actions that are similar can have similar outcomes. Your intention differs from Marjorie's. You don't intend to do harm. Marjorie did. You have a heart and compassion, and you care for people, but your anger gets in the way. Second, I am sorry that my comment weighed on your mind. I want to be honest, right here." Brenda paused. "These sessions are not about me making you feel better. I will not handhold you or throw flattery at you for no reason. You deserve more than that. Besides, I don't do sprinkles and rainbows. I am not a unicorn who shoots stars out of her ass, either. I am honest, direct, and determined to help you manage your anger. Any angry reactions you have, you need to write them down. Did you?"

"No."

"Did you use your one-word answers or journal this weekend?"

Kit said nothing.

"This is a process, Kit. It takes time."

"Yeah," Kit said.

"Glad you're using the one-word answers. They need to be used outside this office. Here we must communicate."

"It's okay for you to give me only one word, but I can't?"

"Yup."

Kit grunted.

"I'm going to give you time to reflect upon that. Did you read the book I recommended?"

"No. It sucked, and it made me angry. It made me angrier."

"How much of it did you read?"

She shrugged her shoulders. "About three pages."

"Try it again. Give it a chapter or two. Besides being angry at me, my one-word answers, and the book recommendation, how has your anger been?"

Kit picked at the arm of the chair. "I didn't feel angry, mostly sad. I got into an argument with my friend. She was so mad at me. Plus, I felt like I harmed people around me, getting them in trouble with the cops. But I did clear Brian, so that was good. Sarah and I are talking now. That's why I was in a good mood until now."

"Those experiences you had have not changed. You can still be excited about them."

Kit shrugged.

"What did you and Sarah argue about?"

Kit told her the story about the meeting and the talk they had too.

"She said you run away when you get angry? What do you think?" Brenda asked.

"I guess she's right. I only do it so I won't say things I'll regret."

"You handle your emotions by running. Sarah handles them by getting overly emotional. See, we are imperfect people doing what we know." Brenda wrote a note on her pad. "The next time, just listen. Nothing else. What were you going to say to Sarah that would have made her more upset?" Brenda asked.

"That she was an idiot for getting mad about me lying."

"Is she an idiot?"

"No. She was upset. I wasn't being a good friend."

Brenda put her hand up. "You made a mistake. That doesn't mean you're not a good friend. We learn what friends need by talking. There was a lack of communication. No one is bad here."

Kit grinned and twirled her hair. "Thought you didn't want to make me feel better?"

Brenda shook her head. "What's going on with the murder?"

"Craig and Brian are no longer suspects. I don't think it will get solved soon. It has us all on edge. I think I'm missing something. I can feel it."

"I'm not promoting investigating murders, but you have good intuition. Take a break from it. Something might jog your memory," Brenda said.

"Maybe," Kit said as she winked at Brenda.

"Keep up the one-word answers, journal, and read that book I suggested. We'll meet next week."

"Yup," Kit said as she walked out.

CHAPTER 49

Tess stopped by the café in the morning. Kit could see Tess and Sarah chit-chatting through the window as she took the size and specifics of the new coffee maker the team wanted. For a moment, she forgot they knew each other, but then again, Tess and Kit were together all the time before Kit left.

Tess was being her animated self—loud—as she used every part of her body to get her point across. Men flocked to her, and women wanted to be like her. It was her wavy blonde hair, plump frame, and Southern charm that pulled them in. Kit looked over the coffee parts size chart, got a few happy thumbs-ups, and left the café with a coffee tray. From across the Feline Foyer, she heard Tess shout, "Gurl!" to Sarah and saw Sarah blush.

Must be about men.

Tess ran up to Kit, grabbed a coffee, and gave her a kiss on the cheek. "Hey, sweetie, how are you doing?" She rubbed Kit's arm.

"Not bad, actually," she said as she handed Sarah a coffee. "I ordered that coffee maker you asked for."

Sarah did a fist pump. "Sweet!"

"I have five coffee makers at home. I could give you one if you need it," Tess said.

Sarah giggled. "This is an industrial maker. We're getting busy and need a third one."

Tess changed the subject. "So do we know who killed the bitch?"

Sarah giggled again. "God, I've missed you," she said as she half-hugged Tess.

"Nope. But—" Kit looked around and whispered. "I have pictures."

"Pictures!" Tess shouted.

Kit shushed her. "Keep it down. Yes. I forgot to mention them. I took them the night of the murder."

"We need to figure this out. Let me see them." Tess put her hand out.

"Not here. They're graphic."

"Can we get together and go over all the clues we have? You guys can look at the pictures. I don't like blood, but two blondes and a redhead are better than one," Sarah said.

"I don't know." Kit bit her lip. "The detective doesn't know I have these. What if I'm wrong again?"

"What if you're right?" Tess said.

"Yeah, I can't live in fear of this monster picking us off one by one," Sarah said.

"I wouldn't worry, Sarah. I'd be the next one. I live here."

"Come on, Kit. Let's try to figure this out," Tess begged with blue eyes.

Brian walked up at that moment, and Sarah told him the plan.

He shook his head. "You girls are on your own. The detective will lose his shit if he finds out what you're doing. No way. I've seen him in a different light. The under-inspection light bulb."

"Come on," Tess urged.

"This is serious. Please don't do this." Brian looked directly at Sarah.

She met his eyes. "We need to know what happened. It's scary being here alone when a murderer is loose."

"Well, I'm out of this club. Be careful." He walked away.

Kit inhaled. "Alright, meet me at my apartment tomorrow evening around six."

Tess jumped up and down. Sarah gave her a high five.

"And don't tell anyone. Please," Kit said as they all closed their lips tightly.

Kit had a great day. She felt like she'd gained back a bit of control over her life. She organized the office with Sarah. They put up a bookshelf, added a few standing plants and on the back wall, they set Kit and Sarah's desks side by side. They left a round table and chairs in the middle of the room. The couch was under the window that faced the café. Under the window facing the PP Parlor, there was now a long table with an in-box and more plants. There was even a jar of candy for staff to grab.

Sarah and Kit sat at the table and rested.

"What do you think?" Kit said.

Sarah looked around. "This is amazing. I can't believe I have a place to work now. With that safe and the boxes gone, it's spacious."

"Yeah, that safe was old. Glad it's gone. The only thing the office needs is some paint."

"Oh." Sarah's eyes lit up. "We can pick out paint this week."

Kit held up her bandaged hand. "Maybe this month, but not this week."

Sarah nodded. Kit reached over to her desk and picked up an envelope. She pushed it in front of Sarah.

Sarah looked at it and put her head on the table. "Oh, yeah. The Cats Gone Wild sale is in two weeks."

Kit smiled. "Yup. This was your boyfriend's idea."

"He's not my boyfriend!"

Kit laughed as she pulled the laptop closer, opened it, and adjusted the camera. "I think we should call Nan."

"Oh, I haven't talked to her in a while. She's going to love this office."

Kit opened Zoom, and a moment later, she could hear her grandmother quieting everyone down around her, her nose in full view.

Kit made a face. "Nan, lean back. I don't need to look up your nose."

Her grandmother adjusted and smiled. "Is that Sarah Bean? How are you, dear?"

"I'm good, Nan. How's your cruise?" Sarah asked.

Nan looked over her shoulder at the two other women waving as they held up drinks. They all beamed. Nan laughed at them.

"You're getting a tan, Nan. Hey, I rhymed!" Kit said.

Nan put her eyes close to the camera. "Where are you two?"

"Jeez! Nan, back up. I'll show you." Kit pushed the computer around slowly, showing her the office.

"That looks magnificent. Tossed out Marjorie's junk. Splendid! Speaking of her, did they find her killer?"

Kit shuddered. Something about a Brit saying the word *killer* sounded so...Alfred Hitchcock.

"No."

"Bloody hell. You should get on it." Nan took a drink from a woman behind her. "How are Brian and the cats? How is my Miss Gabby?" She took a sip.

They filled her in on Brian, Miss Gabby, and her sock.

Kit noticed the group behind Nan getting bigger. Five people were trying to get into the camera frame. Most were in bright flowered shirts, shorts, and visor hats. Not one looked under seventy, except for Nan. In the middle, a young man sucked up the attention. He was overly tanned, and his shirt looked smaller than it should be. He looked out of place among the pale women. Nan would call him a "handsome bloke."

Nan shouted at them to back off. They dispersed in the background, all touchy-feely with the young man.

Kit readjusted the camera so Nan could see both her and Sarah. Kit caught Sarah's eye.

Sarah mouthed, "What?"

Kit gave her a big grin. "Nan, I want to introduce you to your new cat café manager. That's if she takes the job," Kit said.

Sarah looked stunned.

Nan clapped her hands.

"Sarah, you have been doing this job all along. You would take care of the cat café and the Cat Collectibles shop. Brian will continue to take care of the cats and the PP Parlor. You'll have assistants, of course."

"I-I don't know what to say. I will do my best not to dis—"

Nan shook her head. "Pish! You've been doing this job for years. We want you to get paid for what you do, Sarah Bean," Nan said.

"Sarah, what do you think?"

"Yes!" Sarah said as she hugged Kit.

"Lovely," Nan said. "I wanted to come back this past week when we landed in Puerto Rico, but I couldn't guarantee I would get the flight back before the ship took off again."

"That's okay, Nan. It makes me feel better knowing you are there, safe," Kit said.

Her grandmother put her hand to her chest and turned around to put up one finger. "I got to go. Pablo is going to teach me how to play shuffleboard."

"You know how—"

"Bye. Loves you. Loves you, Sarah." Nan threw kisses and signed off.

Kit turned to Sarah. "She's being coy. She knows how to play shuffleboard, and she's rather good." They both laughed.

"Let's get out of here, go to dinner, and discuss your new job and raise."

Sarah's eyes widened. "Raise? I get a raise?"

"Of course," Kit said as she closed the computer and grabbed her coat.

"Speaking of money, did you do payroll?"

Sarah put her jacket on. "Yes, and I did Brian's."

"See, you're already doing the job." Kit smiled. As they walked out, they talked about adding the Cats Gone Wild to the newsletter and holding a meeting at the end of the week to tell the staff about Sarah's promotion.

"I want this event to be big," Kit said as she passed by the window to the gift shop. The woman at the cash register waved, and they both waved back as they walked out arm in arm.

CHAPTER 50

S arah and Kit dropped three bags on the table. Snacks and supplies for the night.

They cleaned up the small desk near the apartment's front door to put up a large whiteboard, then added markers, colored paper, and a few file folders.

Kit printed off pictures of the crime scene as Sarah put together a cheese plate and bowls of snacks. Despite the murder, this was fun to Kit. Mysteries were her thing. Reading them, solving them, and learning about them.

Not sure how the graphic images would affect her, Kit kept the pictures away from Sarah.

Sarah and Kit gave each other a look. Kit smiled. "You sure you want to do this?"

"Well, I would rather do this than nothing. I can't handle not knowing who killed her."

"Okay," Kit said, looking at the board. She put the printed images in a folder.

There was a knock on the door, followed by a "Hey" as Tess walked in, followed by Brian.

"I found this guy hovering outside your door," Tess said as she gave Kit and Sarah a hug.

"Nice digs," Brian said.

"Where's the wine?" Tess asked, already getting a wine glass out of the cupboard.

Kit pointed to the bottles on the table.

"Thought you weren't coming," Sarah said with half a smile.

"Yeah, well, I'm here for protection. Someone has to keep you girls in check."

"Um-hum," Kit said.

Sarah slid over and looked up at him. She pointed at his chest. "Curiosity made you come back, cat man?" She walked away.

Brian grinned and sat down on the couch, which was positioned to face the board. Tess handed Brian and Sarah each a glass of wine and put Kit's on the coffee table. She sat in the recliner, tucking her feet up as she rocked back and forth.

Sarah sat on the couch next to Brian. He smiled.

"Yeah, doggie, this is exciting!" Tess said, rocking in her chair, gulping her wine.

Kit threw a dry eraser at Tess and began.

"I appreciate you guys helping. Maybe we'll have something to give Detective Flowers. Maybe not. Before we begin, I have pictures of the crime scene." She held up the folder and eyed everyone.

Brian opened his mouth but said nothing.

"The detective doesn't know about them. If you don't want to look, I understand."

Tess leaned forward, almost tipping out of the chair. "Let me see 'em."

Brian shook his head. "I'm not sure if I can handle looking at pictures of a dead body."

Sarah looked him up and down. "Really? You live on the Hallmark Channel."

"Hallmark. Cozy mysteries. Nothing bloody. That's why it's called a cozy mystery."

Tess rocked some more. "Yup, no cozy here."

Sarah shook her head at Brian. "You're weird." She looked at Kit. "I don't want to see them either, but it's important." She rubbed her hands.

"Before we go through the pictures, let's go over what we have. Brian, sorry, but I need to put you up here just to eliminate the clues we have," Kit said.

He frowned. "Yeah, no problem."

Kit eyed the timeline. "Marjorie died around eight-thirtyish, according to the detective. I found her around tenish.

"Lots of -ishes," Tess said.

"Yeah, unfortunately I don't have the coroner's report. Can I continue, Tess?"

Tess lifted her glass toward Kit.

"I found the deceased in the break room with a knife sticking out of her back. Slumped forward on the floor in front of the table. Gabby was playing with the knife, batting it back and forth. Trunk was licking and rolling in the frosting on the table."

Sarah made a face. "Eww."

"Eww is right. The door was closed, too," Brian said.

"Yes, the door was closed."

Tess looked at the board. "Were there any prints on the knife?"

"Good question. No prints, but there was catnip, cat fur, and smudges."

"Smudges?" Tess asked, getting up to get more wine.

"Your guess is as good as mine. We'll look at the murder scene in a few. Let's talk about suspects," Kit said.

Tess came back with a glass of wine and a bottle. She topped off Brian's glass while Sarah put her hand over hers.

"Janice told me she heard Craig and Marjorie arguing. Since the side door to the parking lot is always open, she didn't hear Craig leave. When she went to leave, she peeked into the break room and found Marjorie—"

"The door was open?" Brian asked.

"Yes. She realized Marjorie was dead and freaked out. Saw the catnip and cookies on the table. She took them, closed the door, and put them in her locker. Two days later, she broke into the café to get them out of her locker. She was afraid Craig did it, so she wanted to protect him."

"Maybe she did it?" Sarah said.

"Maybe." Kit pointed the marker at her. "Her prints were on the catnip and cat cookie bags, but then we know she took them. Her prints weren't in the room or on the knife. Craig wore gloves. The only prints were Brian's on the money bag. Sorry, Brian."

Brian rolled his eyes. "Figures."

Sarah leaned into him and giggled.

"Why did Craig wear gloves?" Tess asked.

"The cat treats are sticky," Kit said.

Tess nodded. "What is the motive for killing this bitch?"

Kit pursed her lips and looked at Tess.

Tess looked around. "Oh, come on, it's no surprise that everyone hated her. Dang. Even I heard about all the crap she did. It wasn't no secret."

"Let's not speak ill of the bitch," Kit said.

Tess giggled, almost spitting her wine out.

Turning back to the board, Kit pointed to the word *motive*. "Well, we know Craig was being blackmailed, and Janice was being quasi-blackmailed into giving information—"

"Blackmailed over what?" Tess asked.

"He was stealing cat food from his job and using it to make cat treats."

"Cat food, seriously? He couldn't get it at the store," Tess said.

"High-end cat food. The shit is expensive. His uncle is his boss, his mom's brother. So they won't fire him. Except for that, he's a good kid, just not too business savvy," Sarah said.

"Nice to have someone in high places," Brian said.

Tess laughed as she jumped up to get more wine.

"So how did Marjorie find out about this?" Brian asked.

"She overheard Janice and Craig talking about it. Janice worked at the warehouse for a bit. I found a note that said, 'Leave me out of this,' in Janice's handwriting. She told me everything. I think she likes him."

Sarah nodded. "Looks that way."

"Another motive is opportunity. The back door was open, and of course, no one liked her," Kit said.

Brian looked around. "Well, I don't have a motive. She was a bitch, but we all knew that. I just did my thing."

"Yes, Brian, we'll move you off the suspect board. Miss Gabby proved your innocence," Sarah said as she touched his arm. Brian smiled.

"Gabby?" Tess asked.

Sarah told Tess about the tracking device.

"The night of the murder, Craig said he brought her the cat cookies and catnip to show her the new recipe. She tasted it."

Kit noticed Tess making a face as she walked back to her seat.

She continued. "They argued over pricing. She refused to pay. When he left, he ran over Gabby's sock with his dolly. The marks were the same, plus there was catnip and frosting on the sock. We knew Marjorie was diving into that cake, my cake, making a frigging mess all over the place. Then the cats made a mess."

"Well, Marjorie had those T-rex arms. Hard to get the cake to her mouth," Sarah said.

Brian and Tess roared. Kit chuckled.

"But no blood?" Sarah said.

"Nope," Kit said.

"So Craig left?" Sarah asked.

"Marjorie never closed the door to do payroll. She liked it when the cats came in. Would toss loose catnip on the floor. The housekeeping staff hated cleaning after her," Brian said.

"That's why I never looked in the break room. I wish I had. Maybe I could have helped. I found the bag of money in the hall and figured she had dropped it. So I opened the office with my key and put it in the safe. The wrong slot. Later, after they questioned me, I figured the murderer took it, dropped it, and had to leave because they heard me coming."

"Or maybe it fell and got kicked into the hallway," Kit said.

"You couldn't have saved her, Brian. Besides, how would you have handled all that blood?" Sarah asked as Brian shrugged.

"The detective told me that Marjorie's and my fingerprints, and the frosting and blood, were on the bag," he said.

"Craig wore gloves," Tess said.

"Yes, always, especially handling the cookies," Kit said.

Tess shook her head.

Kit took a sip of wine and looked at the board. "We know she was eating cat treats and had cake. Plus, the catnip Craig brought was all over the floor."

"Anyone want more wine?" Tess asked. Everyone nodded, including Sarah, who only had half a glass.

"Let me get this straight." Brian stood up.

"Marjorie is stabbed by someone. They left all the money behind. Or maybe they grabbed the money bag but got frightened and dropped it when they heard me with Gabby." He looked at the board.

"Yes." Kit sighed. "Are you ready to look at the pictures?"

Brian shook his head and sat back down. "Nope. Not me."

Kit took them out of the folder and spread them across the table. Tess was the first one there, inspecting each one. Sarah hung back, frowned, but then looked at one or two of the pictures. Brian stayed on the couch.

"What is that?" Tess asked, pointing to a picture.

Kit picked it up to look. "A smudge on the wall." She shrugged.

"Was that there before the murder?" Tess asked.

"I think the microwave was covering it, so not sure. No one really used the break room around here. We need to look at it closely," Sarah said.

Brian had his feet on the coffee table, scrolling through his phone. "You guys go. I'll stay here with the wine."

Tess scowled at him. "Don't drink it all. I'll want some when I get back."

"Grab the pictures, Tess," Kit said as she left the room with Sarah behind her.

Tess's eyes went big. "Oh, I'm going to take the other bottle of wine since someone is hogging one of them." She scrunched her nose at Brian.

He cheered her on with his glass, never taking his eyes off his phone.

CHAPTER 51

They moved down the hall, giggling loudly. Tess made T-rex noises, and Sarah tried to grab the bottle with T-rex arms. Kit laughed so hard she had to lean against the wall.

Entering the break room, Kit spread the pictures out on the table while Sarah moved the microwave. Tess held on to the wine, slowly putting it down.

"Yup, here it is." Sarah pointed.

Kit looked. "It might not have to do with the murder."

"That is a big smudge. I would have seen that before. I know I would," Sarah said.

Tess leaned over the table, looking at the pictures. "This is a high table. Didn't look that big in the pictures."

"They're like those in the Foyer. You were there yesterday," Sarah said.

"Yeah, but I wasn't leaning on them, Miss Sarah."

"They call them bar tables."

Tess looked at Sarah sideways. "I know my bar tables, my bars, and my wine, gurl."

Sarah smiled. "Touché. We had too many of them out in the Feline Foyer, so we moved a few in here and replaced them with those smaller tables and chairs."

"Let's recreate this scenario," Kit said.

"Oh, that sounds like fun! Okay, Sarah, you're Marjorie," Tess said.

"Me! Why me?"

"You're about her height," Kit said.

"Fine. Where do you want me?"

Kit moved the table around, opened the door, pushed back the microwave, and moved the seat. She put Sarah at the table. Talking to herself, she continued to move a salt and pepper shaker to where the knife was. Tess's overstuffed pocketbook was the cake.

"Hmm." Hands on hips, Kit looked at the scene from behind them.

"Hmm what?" Tess asked.

"It's really creepy sitting here, Kit," Sarah said.

"I know. Hold on a minute."

Tess handed Sarah the wine. "This will help."

Kit left the room and stood in the hallway for a moment as she looked up and down. She headed toward the open area of the foyer.

A few minutes later she returned carrying Trunk. She struggled to speak, gasping.

"This...cat...is heavy."

She plunked Trunk on the table.

He sat down and stared. "Sit. Sit. Sit."

"Yes, my friend. Sit, sit, sit."

"What?" Sarah asked.

Kit, not realizing what she'd said, ignored Sarah's question. "I'm thinking. Sarah, do me a favor. Stand up and move over here."

Kit stood near Sarah, moved the cat and the pocketbook, and ran her hand along the edge of the table. She kissed Trunk on the head. He closed his eyes and purred. She could hear, "Sit. Sit. Sit." again but faint.

"Yes, that's it!"

Gabby entered the break room.

"Whatcha doing?" She leaped onto the table.

"Figuring out who killed Marjorie," Kit said.

"Talking to the cat again," Sarah said as she sipped her wine.

Tess walked over to the other side of Kit and whispered, "Are you going to tell her?"

"Tess, I can hear you. I'm right here. Tell me what?"

Kit looked at Tess, then moved away with her head down. She took a few sips of wine.

Sarah plopped back into the chair. "Tell me what?"

"It would help the investigation, and you should stop hiding your gift," Tess said.

"Tess, I am trying to figure out a murder. Stop it," Kit said.

"Tell me what!" Sarah said, almost shouting. "I am not letting this go."

Kit sighed and ran her hand across her face. Gabby looked at her. "Go on. I am looking forward to watching her freak out. I could use that cardboard popcorn right now." Gabby sat down.

Kit glared at Gabby, then pulled a chair up to Sarah and sat there for a minute. "We talked about not having secrets. Well, I have a big one." Kit twisted her hair.

Tess kicked her chair. "Kitty Cat, tell her, or I will."

Kit sighed deeply. "I can hear the cats talk."

Sarah's eyes opened wide. "Me too. They meow all the time, especially Gabby."

"I have a lot of important things to say," Gabby said.

"No, I can hear *words*, talking. Like what me and you are doing right now."

Sarah stood up. "You two are messing with me. And you're doing it now while we're looking at murder scene photos."

Tess walked over to Sarah and crouched down. "It's true, sweetie. She has a gift. She ignored it for years. Hard to ignore a gift when it's purring in your face," Tess said and looked over at Kit.

Kit felt her stomach turn as she waited for a response. *Knowing Sarah—*

"So you've been lying to me again?" Sarah said.

And there it was, Kit thought. "No. I tried to tell you yesterday, but you left. Remember? I said I had something to tell you."

Sarah chugged her wine. "I thought you were going to whine about your anger issues. But this? You can't be serious?"

"Whine about my anger issues?" Kit said, surprised.

"Well, you do whine," Gabby said, looking away.

"You're not helping, Gabby," Kit said. Sarah just looked on.

"Did Gabby just say you whined?" Tess laughed and noticed Sarah turning pinkish. "Are you okay, Sarah?" Tess put her hand on her shoulder.

"You can hear them too?" Sarah asked.

"No, I just know Gabby. She complains a lot," Tess said.

Sarah drank more wine. "So if you can hear the cats, why don't you ask them who killed her?"

"It's not that easy. Not all of them talk," Kit said.

Gabby looked at Sarah and then back at Kit. "I told you I saw the boot."

"What? No, you didn't," Kit said.

"Yes, I did, but you never listen to me."

"No, Gabby, you didn't."

"I didn't?" Gabby looked around. "Maybe I didn't. But you still don't listen to me."

"Well, if you didn't talk so—"

"Hey, gurls! Can you stop doing that? It's like following a phone call. We're only hearing one side of the conversation. What's going on?" Tess said.

"Spill, Gabby," Kit said.

Gabby told her what she saw. Kit leaned on the table, listening. Feeling her vision tunnel, she held on tight to the table. Other voices in the room faded. She could barely hear her name being called.

Gabby shouted as she jumped out of the way. "She's going down."

Sarah moved in front of her. "Are you okay, Kit?"

Kit lifted her eyes up to Sarah.

"I should be the one fainting, not you. I just found out you talk to cats. What happened?" Sarah said.

Tess leaned in to steady Kit.

"I know who killed Marjorie."

Tess tightened her grip. "Who?"

Kit shook her head. "No. I can't say. Not yet."

Sarah lifted her hands and dropped them quickly again. "Why not?"

Kit bit her lip. "I have no physical proof. What am I going to do, Sarah? Call the detective and tell him I found his witness? And then hand him two cats?"

"I am more than a cat," Gabby said as she jumped into Kit's lap.

Kit patted Gabby on the head.

Trunk moved closer to Gabby. He rolled over, and Kit rubbed his belly until he jumped down and left the room.

As he walked out, she heard, "Sit. Sit. Sit."

"I feel like I am in a game of charades," Sarah said as she rubbed her temples.

"You and me both, doll. Get used to it," Tess said.

Kit got her bearings and stood up. Sarah walked over. "This is a murder investigation. Just tell the detective about your gifts."

"No! No one can know. No one, Sarah. No one. Not even Brian."

Sarah looked down.

"I went through hell as a kid with these gifts. Everyone thought I was crazy," Kit said as she made circles around her left ear. "Tess was the only one who believed me."

"I'm sorry that happened to you, Kit. It's not something that's normal. It's kinda freaky. I still can't believe it. Not that I don't believe you. It's just hard to believe."

"I know, Sarah. If it gets out, all the people who want to see it in action will be here. I'll have every cat person bringing their cat in to talk to me. It would be a nightmare."

"I won't like that," Gabby said.

Kit smiled at Gabby. "Me either, girl."

"What did she say?" Sarah asked.

"She doesn't want all those people here."

Tess whispered in Sarah's ear. "I didn't really believe her either. I liked her and wasn't one to judge. But then she proved it one day. I lost my shit. You handled it much better than me, Sarah." She giggled.

"I'm not handling crap. I'm tipsy from the wine and kind of numb to all of this. Ask me tomorrow what I think," Sarah said as she leaned into Tess.

"What's going on?" A voice boomed from the door, startling them all.

"Dagnabbit Brian! You walk like a cat," Tess squealed, clutching her chest.

"Brian!" Kit heard Gabby say as the cat dug her feet into her legs and leaped to his chest. Kit winced.

"My Brian." Gabby nudged her face in his beard.

Kit and Sarah caught their breath. Kit looked at Sarah, and she nodded.

"Sorry to startle you all, but I've been waiting back there for a while now." Brian rubbed Gabby's head.

"I think I've stumbled onto something. I need to have the detective bring the knife by," Kit said.

"Oh yeah? What did you find?" Brian asked.

"Um. I can't say yet."

"Why not?" He looked around at everyone.

Tess and Sarah shrugged. "She won't tell us either."

Tess poured the last of the wine into her glass.

Sarah took another gulp, finishing her glass as she almost tipped over. "Shit, too much wine. Can I get another?" She laughed.

Tess linked her arm in Sarah's. "I have a hidden bottle at Kit's. Let's get it."

"Are you joining us, Brian?" Sarah said.

"Nah. I have other things to do. You girls aren't driving, right?"

Sarah nodded. "Nope."

"We are having a sleepover," Tess said.

He nodded at Sarah as he left the room with Gabby on his shoulder.

Kit looked shocked. "We are?"

Sarah and Tess smiled.

CHAPTER 52

T he night seemed to never end. The girls stayed up,
drank, ate, and laughed about the situation, despite it
not being all that funny.

Sarah seemed a bit frazzled at times as she peppered Kit
with questions about her gift, but Kit's mind was on the
murder. Tess jumped in and answered them as she could.

The girls left in the early morning before Kit got up. She
heard Sarah telling Tess, "If you say 'gurl' one more time, I
am going to hit you."

Tess rolled out a laugh. "Gurl, you couldn't hit the side of
that wall right now unless you walked into it."

Kit smiled and drifted off as the door shut, hearing them
banter on.

Midmorning, she chose a small table in the corner of the
cat café. People-watching was one of her favorite pastimes.
It was hard in the café because most people wanted to
speak with her now that they knew who she was. In the
corner, tucked in the back by the bathroom, she could
observe everyone doing their own thing. She noticed a few
joggers on the bike path, but returned to the folder on the

table. She slid a few pictures out to look at them again. Today there was no anger, just sadness.

Sarah sat in the chair in front of Kit.

"You look lovely today," Kit smirked.

"Yeah, that wine kicked my butt. I heard you guys this morning."

"There is no quiet-inside-voice with Tess around. Sorry about that."

Even with a hangover, Sarah was beautiful. The light from the window softened her blue eyes, and her hair, golden blonde, shimmered. Plus, she was so kind.

"Kit, I want to apologize," Sarah said, breaking Kit's attention. "So much has happened. You started over from across the country, had court cases, then Marjorie's death, dealing with all the staff and cats, and then me. I didn't make it easy on you. No wonder you left to go back to your apartment that day. I can't imagine how hard it is to hear the cats, but not say anything to them, or ignore them in a conversation. I'm sorry. I was selfish."

"Sarah, I can handle the cats talking. It's the humans I'm not good with. I shut down when people around me get emotional. If I don't walk away, well, you know what happens."

Sarah looked out the window. "Yeah, I've seen you struggle. Then I hand you a cat."

"Actually, handing me a cat is the best thing anyone has done for me. Not all of them talk, but they are all a comfort when I'm mad. You don't need to apologize. I should have told you sooner, but it's not a straightforward conversation.

Sarah, very few people know about my gifts. I can count on one hand the number of people I've told." Kit leaned in closer to Sarah. "You should be happy that I can now tell you what the cats are saying about your butt."

Sarah gasped. "Really? Do they talk about my butt?"

Kit smiled. "No. Just teasing."

Sarah rolled her eyes and leaned back. "So, are you going to tell me who killed Marjorie?"

A young girl walked up to give Sarah a hug and to congratulate her on her promotion.

"How did they find out so fast? The cats have big mouths." Sarah winked at Kit.

"We're in a café. Everyone talks," Kit said.

"Well...Marjorie's killer?"

"No."

"Damn it." She got up from the table, looked back, and grinned. "You can't blame a girl for trying."

That one-word answer worked, Kit thought.

She got up and went to the patio to call the detective.

"Yes, Kitty."

It's Kit, she thought, but didn't correct him.

"Hi, Kale. I think I know who killed Marjorie."

"You do, huh?"

"Well, I have an idea who killed her, but I need your help. You there?"

She heard a faint sigh.

"The last time we met, you tossed me out of the café. You were rude because I interviewed your friend based on a clue you gave me. Now, you want me to drop everything and come down to go over your thoughts on a murder investigation?"

Spinning her hair, she tapped her foot. She could feel frustration building. She wanted to toss the phone and tell him to screw it.

Breathe Kit. Breathe Kit. Remember what Brenda said.

"Yes."

"Kitty, it doesn't work this way. You don't get my help. I get yours. If you have information, then come to the police station and let's talk. If you're holding information that could be vital to this case, I need to know about it now."

"No."

"No? You just said *no*? Are you really going to risk obstruction of justice?"

Her hand reached into the phone, and she pulled him forward by the tie. "Listen to me, you dumbass," she said as she watched him struggle to get away.

She took a long breath and said calmly. "You're being difficult and an ass right now."

"I'm being difficult and an ass? Wow! Really mature. You have been nothing but difficult. You need to go back to your counselor. It doesn't seem to work all that well."

That hurt, but she wouldn't let him know it. She gritted her teeth and said in a quick breath, "I am trying to help you."

"No, you are impeding my investigation."

"No, I'm not. I have the proof, Kale. When you want it, stop by. Oh, and bring the knife too," she said as she hung up.

She muffled a scream into her arm as she felt the overwhelming desire to punch him in the nose.

"Damn it!"

CHAPTER 53

K it reentered the café. It was so loud. In just the ten minutes she was outside, the crowd had picked up. For a moment, she couldn't think as she fought the onslaught on her senses.

How do people concentrate with all this noise? she thought as a group of about a dozen girls walked in. They giggled, laughed, and expressed every emotion in high-pitched voices. It grated on every one of her nerves. She needed to escape back to the Feline Foyer and prepare for them to come into her sanctuary. Luckily, there were rules about loud noises there.

Eww. No wonder I like cats. Kit typed the key code into the Feline Foyer door and walked into an oasis of calm.

"Ahh."

She heard a few cats talking in the back. She even homed in on a few meows as they rolled around, enjoying a belly rub or playing with whatever toy was in front of them.

"What a life," she said as she watched Leanne bounce over.

"Hey, K-Kit!"

Kit put her cup in front of her just in time to block a hug. She noticed Leanne's hair, which was pink now. *Does she rotate the colors? Are they random? We need to chart this,* she thought. "How's Peanut Butter?"

"H-he is g-great!" She pulled out her phone and put it in Kit's face. It was a picture of Peanut Butter leaning back on a couch with a sparkling blue hoodie on. He looked content.

"Hoodie, huh?"

"Y-yeah, he loves it. S-so cozy," she said, looking at the picture and giving the screen a kiss.

"Good. I'm happy." *Not happy about the hoodie, but the cat is happy.* "Leanne, can you help us out in the Cat Collectibles? We have a big sale coming."

"I s-saw the f-flyer. Y-y-yes, I c-can," she said as she shifted her weight back and forth.

"Great!" Kit walked away, glancing back to see Leanne kiss the screen again.

Trying not to giggle, she said, "Oh, Leanne, you're doing a great job helping Brian."

Leanne's eyes went big. "I h-have a q-question?"

Kit stopped. "Sure."

She looked around and whispered, "Is Brian single?"

Kit coughed as she tried not to laugh. In a serious tone, she said, "I'm not sure, but I think he's dating someone."

Her shoulders slumped. "O-oh."

Kit leaned in. "Listen, I know you like Brian, but honestly, you can do much better. He is emotional and needy."

"Oh. W-well, I a-am independent. I don't l-l-like needy men."

Kit pointed between herself and Leanne. "Us women need strong-minded men." She winked.

Leanne stood up tall. "Y-yes, we d-do," she said as she kissed the phone a third time. Kit wondered how many kisses she gave Peanut Butter in person.

She left Leanne and walked into the PP Parlor. Brian and Peter were pointing to a wall. Peter flinched when he saw Kit.

Brian turned toward Kit. "Hey."

"Just checking in. Leanne is going to lend a hand this weekend," Kit said.

"Good. She's been a big help."

Peter looked away from Kit.

"Hey, Peter." Kit waved.

He barely lifted a hand. "Hey," he squeaked out.

Brian walked over to Kit. "Any insight on the murder?"

"Working on it. I asked the detective to come in today."

"And?" Brian asked.

"He hung up on me. He's being such an a—"

"No swearing in front of the cats."

"You're funny," she said behind her cup. "Like they can hear me."

"I heard that," Gabby said as a few other cats talked, creating a low hum.

"Hi, Gabby! How's my pretty girl?" Kit winked.

"Your pretty girl is trying to have some alone time with her man, but this twerp keeps interrupting me," she said, eyeing Peter. "I want some cat cuddles and a scratch behind my ears." She looked up at Brian.

"Aww, she is so cute," Brian said. She purred.

Peter looked at Brian. "I don't think she likes me."

"I don't," Gabby said.

Kit snickered.

"I gotta go!" She turned on her heel. Brian reached out and grabbed her arm. Surprised, she spun around, and he let go.

"Keep me posted on the murder," he said.

Kit nodded and walked out.

Yup, the Feline Foyer was full of young Girl Scouts chasing cats around. Kit was watching them as she walked and almost bumped into Detective Flowers. Startled, she was instantly nervous.

What if I'm wrong, and I can't explain the clues without giving away my gift? What if–

"Are you here to arrest me?" she said, hoping her voice didn't crack.

He shook his head. "No. Not yet," he said as he eyed the girls. He winced. "Wow, they can get loud."

"Hold on a minute." Kit walked over to one of the cat handlers. She pointed to the group of girls. The cat handler nodded and walked over to them.

"That should help. They're supposed to be quiet in here. It's not a library, but those high-pitched voices can upset the cats and me. You are looking very cop-ish today." She smiled.

"I am a cop," he said.

This is going well, she thought. Taking another sip of her coffee, she settled her nerves. "You're being ungrateful. If I'm right, I removed one less murder from your caseload."

He made a face. "We'll see, Kitty."

"Yes, we will Kale."

They moved into the break room. As they walked by the office, Sarah saw them and scurried to the door, peeking her head out. Janice also peeked her head out. Both of them stood in the hallway, whispering. Kit smiled at them and closed the door. She unlocked the back wall closet and pulled out a folder.

Her palms were sweating, and she felt butterflies swarming in her stomach. "Before I show you this . . . please don't get mad."

"Mad?"

She wrinkled her nose. "Yes, mad. I took pictures of the crime scene," she said as she turned her head.

"You what?!" His nostrils flared.

She put her hand up and spoke fast. "Hear me out. I really think you'll want to see this."

He put his hands on his hips and looked down as he moved back and forth. He inhaled loudly. "This explains the footprints."

"What footprints?"

"There were footprints in an arc about six feet from the body. I figured they were yours as you looked at her, but now it makes sense. You were taking pictures."

"I was looking at her, then trying to shoo away the cats from her. I didn't want to move any closer. Do you know how hard it is to get cats away from catnip?"

He squeezed the bridge of his nose. "I dunno, Kit, this is not cool."

Her voice cracked. "It might be. Especially if you solve the murder."

He looked up at the ceiling.

"There are no clues up there. I looked," she said.

He looked right into her eyes. "This is not funny." He paused. "Let me see them." He held his hand out.

She went to the table and fanned out the pictures. He clicked his tongue. "These are better than the crime tech photos."

"Really?" She beamed.

"Don't get excited. I am still not happy with you."

Kit moved the microwave and pointed to the mark on the wall, then she moved fast to the table and ran her hand along the front edge.

"See this here." She bent down and pointed again. "And this blood spot."

She paused and pointed to one more thing. "This. No one knows about this except for one person."

He looked up at her. "Can you slow down? I can't process all this with you running around like a cat with its tail—"

She shook her head hard. "Nope. We don't talk about hurting cats."

"It was a metaphor."

"I don't care."

"Fine. Continue, but slower."

"I can't slow down. My mind is racing, thinking of all the things. This is terrifying and exciting at the same time and—" She stopped short and closed her mouth tight.

He exhaled and ran his hand across the table. "Walk me through what you think happened, step by step."

She talked him through everything, and by the time she finished, she felt better, calmer.

He rubbed his cheek. "Huh. You might have something here."

"I told you," she said under her breath.

"I heard that, Kitty." He grimaced as he put on blue latex gloves.

He must be intimidating in an interrogation room. He could look right through you. Kit stood still, realizing this was not the time to talk.

He took a few plastic bags from his pocket and removed a small knife from a sheath. Scraping the area behind the microwave, he added a sample to the bag and marked it. Walking out of the break room, he had everyone move out of the way so he could collect more evidence.

"Did you find it?" Kit asked.

"Yes, it was still there."

He pulled off his gloves, put the bags in his pocket, and frowned at her.

Uh-oh.

"How did you figure all this out?"

"A cat."

He smirked. "A cat? Cute." He ran his hand through his hair. "No, seriously. How?"

"A cat," she repeated. "He was sitting right there, and it all clicked."

"The big cat? The one that was stuck in here with her?"

"Yes. Trunk."

He nodded his head. "Okay. I can see how you deduced all of this from that." He bit his lip and shook his head again.

"A cat." He chuckled. "I'm going to take this back to get tested. Don't say a word." He stuck his finger about an inch from her nose. "Keep doing whatever you do around here. I should be back in a day or so."

He scooped up the pictures. "I'm taking these too."

"Aww, come on!" Kit said.

He pointed his finger at her again. *She grabbed hold of it and bit hard. He screamed as the blood dripped down his hand.* She shook her head, letting the image fade away.

"How am I supposed to act normal?"

"Just do what you do. You'll be fine."

"Said the cop who carries a gun." Kit looked at his service revolver.

"First off, I need proof, so I need to test these items. Until then, keep a low profile and don't discuss this with anyone."

"You said that already."

"I wouldn't have to if you listened. Goodbye, Kit."

"Goodbye, Detective Flowers."

He waved the folder at her as he left the room.

She looked down at her phone. *At least I still have the digital photos.*

CHAPTER 54

K it was back in Brenda's waiting room. She wanted to turn her phone off, but today she couldn't. She'd been waiting for the detective to call her since last Wednesday. The situation had put her on edge. Sarah had peppered her with questions every day, and Tess had started texting and calling. They were relentless.

Brenda waved Kit into the room. She sat in her usual chair, fluffed her pillow, and tucked her feet under her legs.

"How have you been doing?" Brenda asked.

Kit moved the hair out of her eyes. She got right into the story about the murder, the detective, and Sarah - minus the cats.

"Kale, huh?"

Kit rolled her eyes. "Yes, Kale. He keeps calling me Kitty, so I call him Kale."

"Was there a reason for naming you Kitty?"

"As I mentioned before, I have an intuitive nudge when it comes to cats. So my Nan named me Kitty." Kit started to twirl her hair.

"Tell me more," Brenda said as she adjusted in her chair and rested her chin on her hand.

"My mother died giving birth to me. Nan moved from England to take care of us." Kit began tracing a circle on the edge of the chair.

"What was your mom's name?

"Catherine or Caddy. They named the cat café after her."

"Oh, I thought the café was named after your grandmother."

"No, her name is Victoria, but everyone calls her Nan. When she was thinking of names for me, she realized our cats flocked to me, never leaving my side. She decided Kitty would be perfect. Plus, my mom loved cats so much. I know very little about my mom. She moved to the United States when she was eighteen. My grandmother stayed in England. They were close, but my mom was private, so she shared little. When my mom had Sky, my grandmother visited. Then after that, their relationship got stronger. Two years later, at twenty-seven, when I was born, she was gone. Sky only remembers her in a white dress, twirling around." Kit paused.

"Nan was fun. We were always doing things outside. My sister was always trying to copy whatever she did. I just watched. I remember we used to talk like her in a British accent, saying 'Bugger' and 'Let's get the lift.' Sky got her accent perfectly. I struggled. We had fun, though." Kit looked down at her lap. She laughed. "At one point, we tried to get Nan to drive on the opposite side of the road so we could be in England."

Brenda was quiet.

Kit continued. "I often wonder if my mom would be proud. My grandmother had to deal with a lot from me."

"How so?"

"I was difficult. A rebel. Both Sky and I were."

"Thanks for sharing these memories with me, Kit."

Kit smiled.

"What about your anger? How has that been?"

"Ahh, not as bad as before. I only visualized hurting, um, three people."

Brenda nodded.

"I did this as a child, you know. I remember getting teased as a kid. I remember imagining getting the better of them. I didn't understand the visual, so I thought I was a bad person who was going to hell."

"Did you ever try to change the visual to something, um, nice?"

Kit turned quickly toward Brenda.

"No. That sounds horrible. I like the satisfaction of watching them squirm."

"So you enjoy the pain of others?"

Kit looked up. "Sounds that way, huh? I don't think so. I just need to release my anger, and these images do that. It's like a kid taking a cookie from the cookie jar. They know it's wrong, but they do it anyway. I like knowing they don't know what I'm thinking."

"Okay, we'll come back to this. A lot to unpack there," Brenda said as she wrote things in her notebook.

"How is your hand? I don't see a bandage."

Kit wiggled her fingers. "Much better. It still aches occasionally, but at least I can use it now."

"I found out something today that you should know."

Kit leaned in. "Okay."

"Ivy, the woman who called me for Judge Fink, had a few interesting things to say."

Kit scrunched her face. "Ivy? Why does that name sound familiar?"

"Apparently, you met her in the bathroom at the courthouse in California. Then she called you, reminding you to call me. Ring a bell?"

"Oh, yeah! The lawyer lady who loves to give advice." Kit rolled her eyes and sat back in the chair.

"She requested to contact you, but she wanted to make sure you were doing okay."

"Why."

"That is something she—"

Kit's phone buzzed. She looked down at it and stiffened in her chair.

"You know you're not supposed to have your phone on, right? Those are my ru—"

"I'm sorry, Brenda." She was white as a ghost.

"Everything okay, Kit?"

"This is the detective. He said I was right about who the murderer is. He wants me back at the cat café."

Brenda scrolled through her phone. "You go. This is the closure you need. I'm heading on vacation next week. Let's meet in two weeks."

Kit nodded.

"Kit, I am proud of you. You are making great progress. Keep your wits today. This may be more difficult than you think it will."

"I will."

Kit ran out of the office, her heart racing. She knew this was the moment that everything at the cat café would change.

CHAPTER 55

K it's legs were wobbly. It was hard putting one foot in front of the other as she entered the Feline Foyer. This was big. This was terrifying.

She went around and gathered everyone who worked in the immediate area to go to the break room. Sarah called Tess, who showed up too.

Peter made his usual comment, "Why is she here?" When Brian looked over at him, he lowered his head and followed everyone into the room.

The break room was small, but with everyone in it, it seemed much smaller. Sarah arrived arm in arm with Tess. Janice followed Peter and Brian. Kit walked in, then the detective and an officer. They remained between the door and table. No one was leaving, that was certain.

Craig ran in and stopped short when he saw everyone standing. Detective Flowers pointed for him to stand near the back wall with everyone else. As he walked by, his eyes darted around.

Kit looked at everyone. The tension was high, and it was getting warm in the room.

The detective looked around and pointed at Kit. "Go ahead, Kit. Tell them what you found."

Her wobbly legs were now like rubber bands, and she knew her voice would crack. She took a deep breath, cleared her voice, and started.

"I have been looking into the murder, and I found a few things that told me without a doubt who killed Marjorie." Kit paused and, for a split second, realized she enjoyed this.

Everyone looked around and started talking until the detective hushed them all. The room went silent.

Kit stood next to the large table. "Marjorie was sitting here. She always did because she could see out into the Feline Foyer. Plus, she could watch the cats come by. She was eating the cake from my party earlier on and drinking wine. Lots of wine."

"Her alcohol level was high," Detective Flowers said.

Kit pointed to the table. "The cake was here, and there was catnip all over the table and the floor. Trunk was on the table, sitting here, probably licking the frosting off the cake."

A few people giggled.

"I believe what happened was an accident. Something made Marjorie get up from the chair, and because she was drunk, she was off-balance. I believe she pushed the murderer into the wall, the murderer pushed her back, and she fell against the table."

"I don't understand. She was stabbed, right?" Sarah said. Peter looked at Sarah and nodded.

"I'll get to that. See this mark on the table? The cake knife hilt made this. Trunk was sitting on the knife hilt. A twenty-pound cat can hold a knife down. Luckily, he didn't get hurt. Marjorie tossed the catnip on the floor and took her shoes off. Since she was in socks, it was slippery. She hit a patch of it when she fell back." Kit looked around at the scene.

"The person who committed the murder knew about this cat door. It was closed after Gabby went in, which it hasn't been in years. This kept the cats in. When the detective looked at the door from the outside, there was a piece of glove stuck in the lever. The cats wouldn't have stayed in the room otherwise. Craig never mentioned Gabby in the room, only Trunk."

Kit walked around the room. Sarah was looking down at the floor while Brian looked over at her. Tess held on to every word Kit said, trying not to show enjoyment on her face.

As she passed Craig, he was looking around the room, fidgeting with the hair tie on his wrist.

Janice was staring into space. Peter was looking at the detective and at Kit.

"The detective ruled out Brian. We have proof that he walked Gabby around at the same time every night. Her tracker proved he never entered the break room." Kit paused in front of Sarah and winked. "Sarah was home."

She took a few more steps. "They cleared Craig from a neighbor's video. Plus, his polygraph was negative."

She stopped in front of Janice. "We know you broke into the café to retrieve the catnip and cookie bags. Your fingerprints were on them. You did that to save Craig from getting accused. But your alibi is questionable."

Janice adjusted her glasses, then put her head down.

Kit took one step and turned to Peter. His eyes went wide, and he squirmed. He glared at Kit. "What about your alibi, Kit?"

"She's cleared," the detective said.

"What does that mean?" Peter asked.

"We cleared her on the night of the murder."

Peter huffed. Kit stood in front of him, making direct eye contact. "You have access to the back room, and no one has questioned you. I'm also wondering why you tried to scare me on the bike path."

Everyone leaned forward to look at him. He shrugged, swallowing hard. "Marjorie was my friend. Everyone joked about her. Then you blamed Brian, and now you think I killed her? I didn't!"

Kit stared at him, watching a bead of sweat drip down his face. He looked away.

"I know you didn't kill her." Kit sighed and turned back around to face Janice.

"Janice, why was your ripped glove in the cat door?" Kit asked.

Janice paled and gasped.

"You knew about the cat door. You told me how loud things sounded in the break room from the hallway if it was open."

The detective walked over and took Janice's phone from her back pocket.

Kit pointed to the dent in the phone case. "The smudge on the wall over there is from this phone. Right, Janice? What happened that night?"

Sarah gasped and covered her mouth. She buried her head in Brian's chest. Tess grabbed onto Craig's arm, squeezing it tight. Peter just stared. No one said a word.

Janice slumped to the floor, sobbing. "It was an accident."

Kit grabbed the chair by the table and placed it near Janice. She helped Janice into the seat.

Detective Flowers looked at her. "You have some explaining to do, Janice."

CHAPTER 56

J anice began her story.

"I walked by and saw her pulling money from the cash register, licking her fingers, and splitting the money into two piles. The money bag was out. She wiped her hands on a napkin, took a few bites of cake, and guzzled her wine." Janice sniffled and took a deep breath.

"I went into the kitchen, and when I came back out, I heard Craig talking to her. He said something like, 'You can't do this. You're ruining my business. Look at all this money in front of you. You have it to pay me what I'm owed."

Everyone turned toward Craig. He nodded.

"How did you hear Marjorie and Craig?" the detective asked.

"The cat door. It magnifies sounds in the room. It was open, so I leaned against the wall and listened. After she grilled him and put him down, she had the nerve to laugh. Who would be so mean?"

Craig sat down in the back. He wiped his eyes.

"I went back into the kitchen but stayed by the door. I can always tell when Craig is coming around. His dolly squeaks. As soon as he left, I walked into the break room."

Janice continued in a shaky voice, "She was sitting at the table. The green bag was there, Trunk was licking cake, and she was drinking her wine. The catnip bag and the cookie bag were behind the open register tray on the table.

I was so mad at her. At first, I figured I would try to talk to her in a calm voice. I told her how I knew she was a kind person at heart and that she didn't realize how much this was hurting Craig. She looked at me and said this was none of my business. But she got me involved when she tried to blackmail me regarding Craig. It *was* my business. She just ignored me and sprinkled catnip on the table near Trunk, which spilled on the floor."

Kit could feel her blood boil. Marjorie really had had no heart. She took a few breaths in and focused on listening.

"She told me I could get fired for protecting a criminal. Craig, a criminal? She was the criminal, taking his cookies and not paying him!

At that point I told her I'd had enough, that I was going to tell Kit what she was doing. She told me to get lost. Go have fun with my boyfriend. I told her he wasn't my boyfriend, but a friend. She laughed again."

Janice took off her glasses. A tear ran down Janice's face as she looked down at her hands. "I've been dealing with her for ten years. Ten years! And she still knew nothing about me and didn't care to."

Sarah moved to Janice's side and put her arm on her shoulder.

"Marjorie waved me off. But I had more to say. I told her exactly what I thought of her. I must have said something that got her real mad because she jumped out of her chair, waddled over to me, looked me right in the eye, and pushed me as hard as she could into the wall."

"That's when your phone slammed into the wall, making the mark?" Kit said.

"Yeah. I didn't think. I just pushed her out of my face, but when she fell back, she slid on the catnip. Her feet flew out in front of her, and she landed hard against the table. Right where the knife stuck out. Trunk jumped back, landing on the cake as she slid to the floor.

At first, I thought she fell. I was going to laugh at her, thinking she'd gotten her karma, but then I saw the blood pour out. I panicked."

"I remember you telling me to watch out for the catnip on the floor when I had my slipper socks on," Kit said.

Janice nodded. "She took her shoes off all the time. When she didn't move, I looked behind her and saw the knife sticking out. At that point, her body had slumped forward. I've never seen a dead body before. I didn't know what to do. I just froze." Janice's eyes were red, her face blotched, and her whole body was shaking.

"How did she die so quickly?" she asked through sobs.

"The blade went into a large blood vessel. No one could have saved her at that point," Detective Flowers said.

Janice put her face into her hands and cried. Tess handed her a tissue.

"I grabbed the catnip and cat cookies because I didn't want Craig to get blamed. I shoved them in my pocket and then moved the microwave to cover the mark."

"What happened next?" Kit asked.

"I heard Brian. He was calling to see if anyone was there. He talked to Gabby like he always does on their rounds. I closed the break room door and hid in the kitchen. He called out Marjorie's name a few times, then entered the office. I didn't know the money bag was there. It must have gone flying when she hit the table.

After I watched him close the office door, Gabby jumped down. She homed in on the catnip in the break room. She pawed at the door, then headed to the cat door. Once she entered, I snuck across the hallway and locked her in. I didn't want her meows to call back Brian. She can get loud, you know. I didn't know I ripped my prep gloves. Then I dropped my gloves in the trash and put the catnip and cat cookies in my locker. I went out through the side door before Brian even left. I got sick on the way home."

She covered her mouth so they could barely hear her. "I Did. Not. Mean to kill her."

Sarah hugged Janice.

Kit put her hand on her back. "You should have said something. The cover-up made it worse than the murder."

Peter gasped. Kit looked up at him. He turned away.

"I know," Janice said as Sarah rocked her gently.

Detective Flowers tapped Kit on the arm. Kit tapped Sarah. She let go as he guided Janice to her feet.

She knew he was tough, but today he had kindness in his eyes. He looked at Janice. "I have to arrest you now. We are booking you for murder. This officer is going to walk you out and give you your rights. Do you understand?"

She sobbed even harder as she nodded her head.

Craig asked the detective if he could go with her. Flowers let him walk out to the police car with her.

As Kit looked around, there wasn't a dry eye in the room. Except for Peter, who scowled at Kit and everyone else.

For a few moments, Kit imagined she could have heard a pin drop. Until Gabby walked in and head-bumped everyone's legs, pulling them out of their trance.

Brian picked her up. She cooed. Kit heard her squeal of delight, talking about "Her Brian" again. He put her on the table, to her dismay. She yelled at him as he left the room, Peter following.

Kit excused herself from Tess and Sarah. She walked out and called for Peter. He turned but looked away.

"I don't know what your problem is with me, but it has to stop."

He glared at her but said nothing.

"Answer her, Peter. I may be your boss, but she's mine," Brian said.

"You think I treated Marjorie badly? No, she treated us badly. Maybe you didn't see it because she was your friend. That's fine. I respect that and your sorrow. But she is not here, and your nasty attitude toward me needs to stop."

Kit's eyes narrowed. "If it doesn't, you can find somewhere else to work."

Kit waited for a minute, but he remained silent. Brian mouthed that he would talk to him. Kit nodded as she squared her shoulders and walked back into the break room.

She could hear them arguing as they turned the corner.

Tess and Sarah stood there. Both were sniffling.

"Everything okay, love?" Tess asked.

"Kids," Kit said with a grin.

"That's why I don't have any spawn," Tess said.

They laughed for a moment then the room became silent.

"How did you know she did it?" Sarah asked.

"Gabby told me about her boots. Janice wore the same boots for years, then stopped. A few days ago, she had them on again. Gabby remembered the laces."

Sarah kissed Gabby on the head. "Good kitty."

Gabby meowed. "Eww, human slobber."

Kit kissed her, too, as she made another face. Tess picked her up. Kit could hear her complaining for a minute until the head-scratching began.

"I also heard Trunk say over and over, 'Sit. Sit. Sit.' He was trying to tell me he had sat on the knife."

Gabby adjusted herself in Tess's arms. "A man of many words. If he wasn't a dingbat, you could have figured this murder out a long time ago."

"Gabby. Not nice. Besides, it took you a while to remember the boots," Kit said with a smile.

"I remembered the boots when we were in the break room, but then I forgot."

Kit made a tsking sound and tickled her belly. Gabby kicked her feet.

"Stop it. You need boundaries, woman." Gabby said.

Kit felt like she could breathe easier, although there was sadness in her heart for Janice.

"I feel bad for Janice. It really was an accident," Tess said as she stuck her face in Gabby's fur.

"What's going to happen to her?" Sarah asked.

"I dunno. She should have said something. She obstructed the investigation and hid evidence," Kit said.

Tess looked at Kit. "But it was self-defense, right? Marjorie pushed her first. That has got to count for something. I agree with what Janice said. It was karma."

"Karma Janice will pay for." Kit ran her hands through her hair, exhaling loudly.

"This is so sad," Sarah said.

"I agree," Tess said.

"Now I need to hire another cook," Sarah added.

"Wow, compassion much?" Kit said with a half smile.

Sarah smiled and shrugged. "Hey, the cat café must continue on."

"Damn, gurl. Those blonde curls and flirty blue eyes hide your sass, for sure." Tess chuckled as she carried Gabby out of the room. Sarah followed.

Kit turned back to look at the break room before she turned off the light and closed the door.

CHAPTER 57

"Gather around, gather around!" Gabby said from their bench in the corner of the Feline Foyer.

"Here we go again," Vee said as she stretched her legs out, leaving another clump of her fur behind.

"You really need a groomer, Vee. Dang, you shed like a dog!" Gabby said.

"We don't talk about dogs here," Daisy chimed in. She flipped on her back as she tried to grab Vee's tail.

"If you grab that tail, Daisy, more fur will fly," Gabby said.

"Why are we here? I could get my belly rubbed." Trunk plopped down in front of the girls.

"I could get a meal. It's about that time," Vee said.

"Will you all just stop!" Gabby stomped her paws.

"Did you all hear that Miss Janice killed Marjorie?" Vee asked.

Daisy looked at Vee. "Who is Janice?"

Gabby blinked a few times. "You live here, people. Smarten up."

"We're cats. How are we supposed to know these people?" Trunk said.

"Actually, we are gods. The humans used to worship us years ago," Mr. Nuggy said as he meandered toward the others.

"They just figured this out. You were in the room, Gabby. You should have figured this out earlier," Vee said.

"I was busy," Gabby huffed.

"Yeah, getting stoned on catnip. You should work on that addiction," Trunk said.

"Listen, people, um, cats. This is important. We are getting another cat next week," Gabby said.

They all sat up straight. The only movement was a piece of Vee's hair that flew by Trunk's nose.

"Ah, another family member. How delightful," Mr. Nuggy said.

"I hope it's a Persian," Vee said.

Daisy looked at Vee. "More fur flying, that's what we need. It's bad enough to find yours all over the catwalk."

"Yeah, but they're soft," Vee said.

"They shed! Listen, I have an announcement," Gabby said, raising her voice again.

"I thought that was your announcement," Trunk said as he padded over to the leg of the bench to give it a quick lick.

"No, that was one announcement. This one is more important. I think we need to make sure we keep the cats and this place in alignment. We can't have it going to the dogs."

"Talking about dogs again," Daisy said.

"As you know, I walk the perimeter with Brian every night. We do our check on the whole place—"

"You don't walk anywhere. He carries you," Trunk said.

Gabby paw-popped Trunk on the arm. "I am talking. Be quiet."

She closed her eyes for a moment, then padded back and forth on the bench with her tail up and head held high. She continued.

"I have entered training to become a ninja cat. We need a leader with powerful skills. A warrior cat who can protect our home and make sure we never have another murd—" She looked on as everyone walked away. "Where are you all going?"

"I'm hungry," Trunk said.

"Good night, Gabby," Daisy said as Vee followed behind her, talking about the new cat. "I really hope he's cute."

Mr. Nuggy stood in front of Gabby. "One needs discipline to fight the battle in his mind before he takes on the battle for others."

She looked at him with an open mouth. She blinked. "Huh?"

He sighed. "A warrior cat is patient, Miss Gabby." He meowed and padded away from the area.

Gabby said nothing as she looked down at Trunk. She shook her head. "At least you listen."

Trunk tipped his head up. "Did you say something?"

"Why are you licking the chair?" Gabby shouted.

"It tastes good." He licked the chair again.

Gabby rolled her eyes and jumped off the bench. "Oh, for cat's sake. We need more than a warrior to get these cats into shape. We need therapy." She flicked her tail at Trunk.

"Yeah, let's start with your catnip issue," Trunk said as Gabby walked away.

CHAPTER 58

K it stood in the parking lot, looking at the building. It had been almost five weeks since she arrived at the cat café.

She pointed to her right. "No, lift it up to the right."

Brian adjusted the sale banner.

Kit found the banner hysterical. It had an image of cats partying with block letters that read, "Cats Gone Wild!" Kit gave Brian a thumbs-up.

Sarah ran out of the building, carrying a cup of coffee for Kit. She stood next to her, shielding her eyes from the sun.

"That looks good, Brian!" Sarah shouted.

"You did a great job getting this event together. We need to take pictures for Nan."

"I'm on it." Sarah started taking pictures of Brian.

"Keep Brian's butt out of the pictures. If Nan sees them, she won't notice the banner," Kit said.

Sarah laughed. "Right. I love Nan. She is so sassy." She shook her hips.

Kit took a few sips of coffee, enjoying the moment.

"Oh, did you see the wall? Above the cat doors outside the PP Parlor? We put up two pictures of Gabby and Trunk." Sarah turned her phone screen toward Kit and zoomed in.

"That is hysterical!" Kit saw two pictures of the cats in prison suits with prison numbers. The words below the pictures read, "Under suspicion of murder."

"I don't think Gabby will like it. She'll complain those black and white stripes clash with her fur. I can hear it now."

"That sounds about right. I love to tease her. Now that I know how she thinks," Sarah said.

"Besides Gabby, everyone giggled except for Mrs. Dandriff. Nothing can take a stick out of that woman's a—"

"Who is Mrs. Dandriff?" Kit asked.

"Kit, pay attention. She was the woman who recently complained that we're running a brothel because two cats were spooning each other."

Kit tipped her head back and laughed. "Oh, her. Why is she here if she hates it so much?"

"Her daughters wanted to get her out of the house. They bring her here every week. They love cats. I think they do it to torment her. She is miserable."

Kit smiled. "Stick Leanne on her. Maybe she'll hug her to death."

"Oh, good idea." She giggled. "I'm going to go help Brian. He still can't get the banner straight.

Kit, I wanted to say thanks. I know this past month has been hard. You stuck it out. I don't know if I said it. I'm glad you're here."

"I couldn't have done it without you, Sarah." Kit gave her a hug as her phone rang.

Sarah let go and bounced off toward Brian.

Kit loved watching Sarah and Brian. He was so tall. She was so tiny. She kept him in check, though. They are going to be good together if he ever made the official move.

Nan popped up on the video.

"Hey, you get the pictures?" Kit asked.

"I did. He needs to straighten that banner. A bit off."

"Yes, Sarah went to help him with that."

"I got the pictures of the cats in prison suits. What a hoot! How is everything going? Feel like it's been months since we talked," Nan said.

"It's been two weeks, Nan. The ocean air is getting to you. It's going to go well. We got Craig making the cat treats. We made him a permanent subcontractor, exclusive to us now. Your suggestion of adding our name to his packaging was great. Caddy & Craig Cat Cookies."

"Good. He's a grand lad. How is Sarah doing?"

"Great. She's adjusting to her new role. She's been interviewing for a new cook, but she's picky. They're managing right now," Kit said.

"Tell Sarah to Zoom me. I may have someone she can interview. I think he would be a great fit."

"I will," Kit said.

Nan lowered her voice. "How is Janice? I got her a great solicitor. I mean lawyer."

"She's okay. She may only get probation or a few months for the obstruction, especially if Detective Flowers can prove it was self-defense, which he thinks he can."

"Good. I'll be heading back in about a month. I need some solid land, and I miss you." Nan sighed. "It's been too long."

"Okay, Nan, I got to go. We're opening our sale in about an hour."

"Loves you. Give the gang a hug for me!"

Kit stood there for a moment and closed her eyes. She felt the sun's warmth on her face, the salty air catching in her throat. She really loved this place.

"Kitty. Good morning."

She opened her eyes to see Detective Flowers standing in her view.

"You're blocking my sun," she said.

He looked at the sign and giggled. "Cats Gone Wild, huh? Don't you think you've had enough excitement for a bit?"

"You should see the mugshot pictures of the cats in the café."

"I'll have to go arrest them."

"Good luck. I heard one of them is a bit feisty."

He paused. "Good point. I'll get some treats for her first, huh?"

Kit smiled. "What brings you down here? You don't have cats."

"I was told I have to make up for my blunder with the cats that were left in your shop, so they forced me to buy a crapload of gifts."

"Who are 'they'?"

"Your staff, including Tess."

Kit hid a smile behind her coffee cup. "You have finally seen the error of your ways. And maybe you should thank me for helping to solve your murder."

"Oh, did I forget to say thank you? Hmm."

"Any time now?" Kit said.

"I'm going to grab a coffee. I'll see you in there?"

"Yup, in a few. You're welcome, Detective Seaweed." Kit watched him walk away. She liked him, not in a want-to-date-him way, but she thought she might have found another friend.

Tess walked up. "Hanging with the detective again, I see."

"You gave him crap about the cat shop?" Kit asked.

"Hell yeah!" Tess said.

"Nan sends you a creepy hug."

Tess laughed. "Speaking of creepy hug, what color hair is that?" She pointed to Leanne standing at the door, looking up at Brian.

"Blue? No. Green? Beats me."

"It's seaweed color. She's doing aqua themes now." Tess held her hand over her face as she giggled.

Leanne waved. They both waved back.

"I really like her. Such a good egg," Kit said.

Tess kissed Kit on her cheek. "Gonna grab a coffee, gurl."

Kit's phone beeped.

She saw a text message from Brenda.

I am looking forward to our session next week. I got lost on vacation, extended it another week. Keep up with your journal. I hope you have a great event today. It must be big. I saw the notice in the paper and on the news. Wow! One more thing. I was hoping to talk to you about this in person, but I won't be back in time. Ivy will call you this week to talk to you. She was good friends with your mother—

Kit read nothing else. She felt excited, overwhelmed, and a bit angry at not knowing about this. But to talk to someone who knew her mom would be priceless. She knew so little about her life.

How did they know each other? When? Oh shit! I was so mean to her.

A pain in her calf broke into her thoughts.

"Ouch!" she said as she turned around to see Peter with a cart against her calf.

She looked at his expression as he stammered. "I'm...I'm so sorry, Miss Kit. I didn't mean to slam into you. Again."

*She slammed the cart back into him, and he went flying. She poured her hot coffee over his head—*she stopped.

"It's alright, Peter. But watch where you're going." She rubbed her leg.

Brian called Kit into the building. Peter followed behind, keeping his distance.

As Kit walked into the building, she felt giddy, knowing that she would get to offer Brian a promotion to cat manager. Little did he know they would add another five cats, and Nan wanted to pay for his veterinarian schooling.

He is gonna explode. Nan has a way of making dreams come true.

She walked in to hear a lot of noise. Today it didn't bother her. Vee and Daisy were looking in the window of Kitty Cat

Collectibles, trying to get in. They even asked the new gray cat to join them. It was a young boy with no name yet, who was not a Persian. Vee was not happy about that. Gabby wanted to name him, but she couldn't decide, or so she said.

Up high, hanging on a cat bed, Mr. Nuggy sat with his paws tucked under his chest. He was so regal on his cushion of contentment, pondering the action below him.

Trunk tried to hide his table- and wall-licking, but Gabby caught him all the time. He even changed his words. He no longer repeated, "Sit. Sit. Sit."

Thinking of Gabby. Kit looked down. She was standing in front of Kit, straining to look up. Kit picked her up and gave her a squeeze.

Gabby enjoyed having a pet before she started in. "I'm not sure about that new cat." She looked over at him. "He seems to have issues. Can't you find a cat who doesn't chase his tail, literally," she asked.

"You're being judgmental, Gabby."

"I have to be. You don't pay attention to the quality of cats you let into this place."

"Well, you're of high quality, Miss Gabby." Kit kissed her on the head.

"Really? That's why you have a picture of me in a striped suit." She blinked. "I have an image to uphold," Gabby said as she jumped down. She stood and stared at the new cat spinning around, chasing his own tail.

"We will discuss this later, Miss HR Department."

Gabby shook her head and bounced away, heading toward a ball that rolled by.

Gosh, I really love that not-so-ninja cat.

Kit smiled before she started thinking about her mother. She would be proud. Nan was proud. Her phone beeped again. Sky, her sister, had sent a message.

Heard you are doing great there. Knock 'em dead. Oops, wrong words. Loves you, Kitty. Kit texted her back, still smiling.

Kit stood in the Feline Foyer thinking how *pawesome* it was to be there.

She said out loud, "I am perfect. Today is purrfect."

KEEP UPDATED

If you enjoyed this book, please leave a review. Thank you!

Keep updated on my latest releases. Join CJ's Newsletter and you'll receive a **FREE** short story about Kit's reason for leaving California. The prologue to this story- Court Ordered Catastrophe.

Plus, you can enjoy some snarky wisdom from Gabby as she shares her blog posts. Type in this link or scan the bar code. https://BookHip.com/CDZHTJH

Scan the barcode

Love Gabby?

A short story is soon to be published. *The Curious Case of Mr. Buttons* is all about Gabby and the gang trying to solve a non-murder mystery.

https://cjreynoldsauthor.com/mr-buttons/

Want more? Hang out with CJ and other members of the community in the Facebook group.

https://www.facebook.com/groups/cjreynoldsauthor

CADDY CAT CAFE FLOOR PLANS

Grab a free large pdf of the plans.

https://dl.bookfunnel.com/fvl098s5v6

ACKNOWLEDGMENTS

You can't write a book in a bubble. I realized that early on. My cats are the inspiration for this book. Each one of them has peppered this book with their silly ways and personalities.

Thanks to my writing group ... Kristy, H, Ruth, Amanda, Caro, Rachel, and anyone else who joined us. You kept me motivated and inspired when I got stuck. A shout-out to Nora and my mom for supporting me and giving me positive feedback. Kristy Bryson, thanks for making my book look like a real book. You are making me a better writer!

Thanks to my wonderful beta readers ... Susan Mc-Carville, Gala Worthey Tray, Nora Donohue Bagorazzi, and Kristy Bryson. Your honest feedback helped this book become a reality. Susan, thank you for being my proofreading eye, you know what to look for "gurl."

To my mentors. Thanks to the 12-week book course with Richard Nongard, Jane Kalmes' Simple Mystery Course, and Sarra Cannon for her Publish & Thrive course. I also tip my hat to Joanne Penn for her podcast wisdom and guidance as an indie author. These courses and classes made my journey to authorship that much easier.

Thank you, advanced readers; you rock. I appreciate your kind words. And to my editor, Ita, thank you for your kindness and good eye for detail.

I dedicated this book to my Dad and Gram. The past year was difficult with the loss of them both, so being able to spend time at the Caddy Cate Cafe' was a delight as these characters began to take on a life of their own. Especially the cats and Gabby, they made me giggle and snort, and I needed that more than you know.

Above all, thanks to my readers for inspiring me and cheering me on ... if it wasn't for you, I wouldn't be an author.

OTHER BOOKS BY CJ REYNOLDS

Curious Cat Case Files Series- *short stories*
The Curious Case of Mr. Buttons - 7/23

ABOUT THE AUTHOR

CJ, aka Cheryl, a former registered nurse turned writer and hypnotist, is the author of Caddy Cat Café Mysteries and Curious Cat Case Files series. A native Rhode Islander with a strong New England accent, she now lives in the mountains of North Carolina. Her love language is humor. Plus, she likes murder mysteries, cats, coffee, and weird synchronicities that boggle the mind.

Send her a picture of your cat—it will make her happy.

Keep a lookout for the non-murder mystery called *The Curious Case of Mr. Buttons*. It's about Gabby and the gang.

https://cjreynoldsauthor.com/mr-buttons/

Join the newsletter and get a FREE short story about Kit's courthouse situation!

https://cjreynoldsauthor.com/newsletter/
HANG OUT WITH CJ!
FACEBOOK https://www.facebook.com/groups/cjrey noldsauthor